The Ojanox

Scream in the Dark

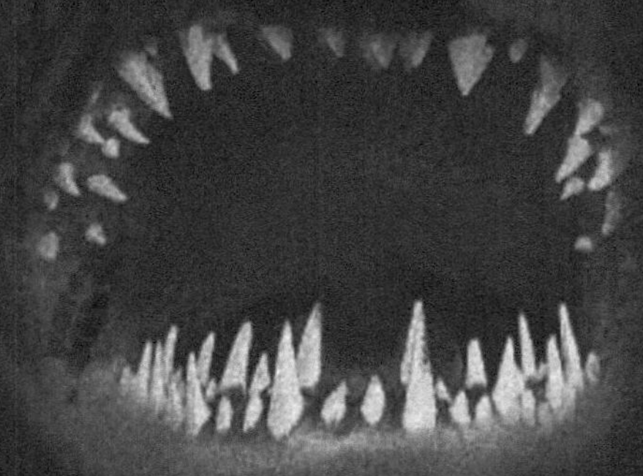

Daemon Manx

Published by Last Waltz Publishing

5 Midland Ave, Pompton Plains, N.J. 07444

www.lastwaltzpublishing.com

Edited by Lisa Lee Tone

Original developmental edits by Ben Eads

Library of Congress Cataloging-in-Publication Data is available.

Robert R. Chiossi, 1967-

The Ojanox Series / Daemon Manx

TXu 2-417-807 2024
ISBN 979-8-9868451-7-3

Also by Daemon Manx

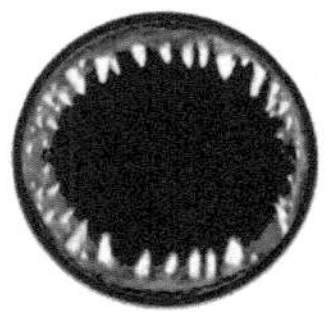

Abigail

Piece by Piece

Drawn & Quartered with Diana Olney

Hacked in Two with James G. Carlson

These Lingering Shadows

Tales from the Monoverse

Arcranium with Mark Towse

Manx-iety: A Collection of Disturbing Stories

The Ojanox Series: I-IV

Scream in the Dark

Ashes to Ashes

All Fall Down

Lonesome Mountain

Praise for The Ojanox

"Every so often, a writer reads a coming-of-age tale that they wish they had written themselves. That's how I felt with *Scream in the Dark*, Book One in Daemon Manx's *The Ojanox* series. Exciting, genuinely nostalgic, and scarier than hell! I can't wait to get my hands on Book Two!" –Ronald Kelly, Author of *Fear*, *The Essential Sick Stuff*, and *Southern-Fried & Horrified*

"In *The Ojanox*, Daemon Manx creates a community and cast of characters you feel like you know personally, like you've known them all your life. And when you lose one of those characters, you've lost one of your own. Manx makes you care and makes you hurt. *The Ojanox* is a masterclass on characterization." – Patrick C. Harrison II, Author of *Grandpappy* and *100% Match*

"*The Ojanox* harkens back to the horror boom of the '70s and '80s, in a very good way. Manx has a knack for creating characters you'll love (or hate) and putting them through the wringer. His dialogue is sharp and storytelling gripping and fast paced. Now that I'm hooked, I need to read the rest!" – Duncan Ralston, Author of *Woom* and *Ghostland*

"Written with beautifully descriptive scenes, *The Ojanox* places you directly into the quaint, small town of Garrett Grove during the Halloween season where everything is pleasant ... until it isn't. An ancient, dark entity is accidently excavated and escapes into the world with chilling results. *The Ojanox* is a fresh, original, plot-driven page turner that I couldn't put down. I highly recommend it and am looking forward to Part Two of this excellent series." – Jeani Rector, Editor of *The Horror Zine*

"*The Ojanox* is a perfect first book in what is sure to be a stunning series. Small-town nostalgic perfection, this coming of age story is unlike any I've read before. Manx weaves his tale of terror through dynamic characters, brilliant dialogue, and a mounting dread that carries the reader from page to page, racing to the climatic end. *The Ojanox* is one to own, and Manx has proven himself one to watch." –Candace Nola, author of *Desperate Wishes*

"Daemon Manx has wrapped up a delicious candy treat that you won't be able to resist gobbling down, razor blades and all. *Scream in the Dark* will put you in the Halloween spirit no matter what time of year you read it. You'll be holding out your plastic jack-o-lanterns for more!" — Jeff Strand, author of *TWENTIETH ANNIVERSARY SCREENING*

"In Garrett Grove, the time for evil has arrived, and in *Scream in the Dark*, Manx serves up scares like Halloween candy—the good kind, too ... full-sized, nostalgic, and satisfying to the end."—Gaby Triana, author of *Moon Child;* editor of *Literally Dead: Tales of Halloween Hauntings*

"Daemon Manx has proven in a short time, he is the real deal. *The Ojanox: Scream in the Dark* is the first in a series of four, where he showcases his skills at character development and world building. And he doesn't mess around. This is a must-read series, and one of the best books I've read this year." –Mike Ennenbach, author of *Cuckoo*

"If you are like me and love horror mixed with great storylines and twisted endings, you must read Daemon Manx. And when you are through, hug the pillow, hide under the covers, and repeat over again, it's only a novel ... or is it???" – Jason Knight - ECW Original

CONTENTS

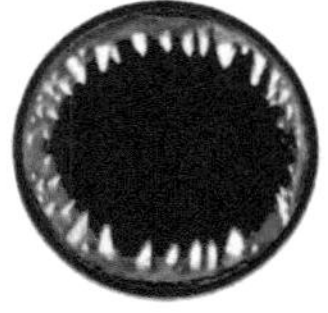

For Mom
The original storyteller

FOREWORD

GAZING INTO THE ABYSS

The year is 1979. A small New York town prepares to welcome the fall season in all the expected ways: young children bicker and boast over Halloween costumes, secret lovers meet in clandestine corners, and a tortured soul plots wicked deeds. All the while, hidden just out of view, patient and hungry ... an ancient evil lurks.

I know, I know. You've heard all this before. You've read the book, watched the film adaptation, and probably even caught the two-part podcast. If you're a fan of old-school horror, like I am, then you'll swear that you know how the plot will unfold. What the primeval horror is. Who will live, who will die, and even in what specific order said deaths will occur.

Hey, I get it. I thought so too.

But I was wrong, dead wrong. You'll probably be wrong too. And, let me tell you, rarely has it felt SO good to be incorrect. To be legitimately surprised. To revisit a hallowed era of storytelling in such a creative way.

Let's be honest: vintage horror is a difficult thing to effectively pull off in today's market. Try too hard and you alienate your target audience, skewing far afield from that elusive "feel". Half-ass it and you're derivative, lazy, or a hefty combination of both.

For anyone who is familiar with his talent, Daemon Manx has, quite unsurprisingly, accomplished something special with *The Ojanox*, making the familiar feel wholly unfamiliar. Pulling us back to the gritty world of late-70s to early-80s horror without stepping on any toes in the process. This is neither an homage nor an emulation. This is a book that could very well have been borne of that halcyon era, resting on some half-askew bookshelf this whole time, just waiting to be discovered. But, as much as *The Ojanox* is a glimpse across decades, it is also a gateway into Manx's mind—one can glean various details about the novelist through the terrors nestled within the typeface.

Much like there are no atheists in foxholes, there are no innocents amongst horror authors. We write from the darkest of depths, from places where light falters and even whispers carry great weight. Yes, the stories we create are ultimately meant to startle, to shiver, and to scare. To invoke those primal sensations of fear and dread. But there is so much more to it than that. We are also, through prose and plot, offering the world a glimpse of our vulnerable sides. Our hopes and fears. The hardships we have endured. Mistakes we've made, and the fallout that followed. From pen to page, our pain is made manifest. Some people suffer for their creations—horror authors put themselves through anguish for their art. And, during this process of composition, this literary baring of souls, we allow ourselves to examine our personal hauntings, be they self-induced or inflicted by others. To exorcise our own demons, keystroke by keystroke. True, we may never completely vanquish the darkness inside us. For many horror authors, those hurts are grafted to our very essence, as much a part of us as blood and bone, woven into the very fabric of who we have become. But, while those shadows may yet linger, we at least get the chance to look our fiends in the eye with an unflinching gaze.

Daemon has never been shy about his personal struggles, of which he has had plenty. I respect both his candor and his fearlessness in facing those dark years. Perhaps that deep well of experience is what gives his writing that extra bit of compelling oomph. Some of us have pint-sized imps on our shoulders, gently reminding us of past indiscretions, tempting us back with honeyed words. Manx has a thousand-pound gorilla clinging to his back, beating its chest and bellowing a mighty roar of misdeeds, yanking at the chains of the past with inhuman strength.

And that, dear reader is what you get with *The Ojanox*. A beast of both the literal and figurative sense. A peek at the demons without ... and those within. This is a massive story, years in the making, touching on a myriad of topics, many of which are just as pertinent today as they were in '79. From a word count perspective (it shouldn't matter, but we're novelists ... it matters) it is an imposing body of work, rivaling the hefty behemoths of the era, as is only fitting. From my first involvement with *The Ojanox*, I have always maintained that Daemon writes like Laymon, but with a more literary bent. This isn't a knock at all: Laymon penned some classics. He was great at concepts, with a knack for the perverse and deft skill at setting a scene. The only place I was occasionally left wanting was with the narrative voice itself. Daemon rectifies that shortcoming with the ease of raw ability, wrangling words in the best of ways. In all honesty, it wouldn't shock me in the slightest to see Manx and Laymon sharing space on bookstore shelves in the not-so-distant future. I am hard pressed to think of an indie author who deserves it more.

But don't take my word for it. See for yourself. Curl up in your favorite space, dim the lights, crack open *The Ojanox*, and step into the town of Garrett Grove. What you find just might surprise you.

Jack Wells

Author of *Jack of All Trades* and the *Monochrome Noir* series.

TRICK OR TREAT

I hope you will indulge me just a little before diving into the book, as the origination of *The Ojanox* is almost as interesting as the story itself. I began the writing process during the spring of 2020 while I was serving my final year of incarceration in a halfway house in Newark, New Jersey. Yes, you read that right. I spent nearly a decade in state prison prior to that. The short story: I made some terrible mistakes because of addiction (rarely are addicts known for making good ones), and that landed me in a very dark place.

But that was only the beginning of my journey because prison is where I finally got clean (Eleven years and four months as I write this today) and it's where I turned my life around. But something else happened while I was serving my days behind the wall. I started writing again. Addiction had stolen everything I loved, and my creative muse was only one of the casualties. But as the fog lifted, my desire to create returned, and it was in a cold, lonely cell where I started to live once again.

By the time I reached the halfway house, years later, I had written dozens of short stories and novellas but had never tackled any larger projects. It was January of 2020, and I had just received permission to leave the halfway house for a few hours a day to attend college in person. I even got a couple months under my belt, and then Covid hit. The house was put under quarantine lockdown, and no one was allowed to leave. Unfortunately, the virus had already found its way into the building.

And that was life for the next seven months. We started out with almost three hundred men in the facility, and that number quickly diminished to less than a hundred. We all got sick during that time, some more than others, and many of the men were taken back to the prison system's medical facilities ... never to return.

To pass the time, I started writing what I thought would be a short story, one that encapsulated the feeling and the mystery of Halloween the way I remembered it as a child. I sat down and wrote the first lines of what is now chapter one, and *The Ojanox* was born. Within a few days, I realized this was not going to be a short story. I had no idea just how massive it would be, but I was about to find out.

I owned a portable word processor called the Alpha Smart 3000, originally intended for my college classes. If you're not familiar, The AS3K is a battery-operated unit with a small screen that allows the user to see three lines of script at a time. There are eight files you can fill with text, but once they are filled, you must transfer the data to a Word doc and zip drive. I would fill the files every night, writing from 6p.m.–11p.m. non-stop. The next day I would use the house's library computer to transfer my work and ultimately free up space for another night of writing.

I should mention that I shared the room with ten other men who were anything but quiet. Who can blame them? We were all stir-crazy. While they were listening to music, playing poker, and screaming to one another in the confines of our 12 x 12 room, I would don my headphones, crank up the tunes, and write, write, write.

And yes, it was like that. I wrote in a fever; the words flowed as if they were coming from somewhere other than me. It was very stream of consciousness, but it was also methodical. During the day, I would map out the next ten scenes in outline, and that night, I would write. Oddly enough, not once did I experience even an ounce of writer's block.

On October 30, 2020, I typed the words *The End* and looked down at a massive file containing 520K words. I had finished the first draft in six months. Seven days later, I was released.

Now would come the hard part. The rewrite. Little did I know, I would be rewriting this beast for the next four years and editing out over 160K words, all for the betterment of the story, I assure you.

Now it's true that this story was created under some very adverse conditions. You could even say it is a byproduct of that suffering. But that's not why *The Ojanox* was written in such a short period of time. To be honest, I have been working on this story since I was ten years old myself. Like Troy Fischer, when I was in fourth grade, I had a Halloween party and built a haunted house in the garage. Yep, you guessed it, it was called Scream in the Dark. In *The Ojanox*, many of the settings, themes, and circumstances are inspired by my memories of Halloweens gone by and my own life experiences as well. However, this story isn't just a tribute to my own childhood but to childhood itself. If I have done this correctly, it is to pay respect to that initial sense of mystery we all felt when we heard our first ghost story, to that chilling fright when we saw our first horror movie.

Although the coming-of-age factor is just a small portion of this story, as *The Ojanox* is pure horror with its fair share of violence, I mention it because that's where it started for me ... when I was a child. My love for horror, that is.

If I got any of this right, I hope you are taken back, if only for a moment, to that innocent time in your life when you set out to grab a pillowcase full of candy on Halloween and returned home with all the peanut butter cups you were hoping for ... and more.

Daemon Manx

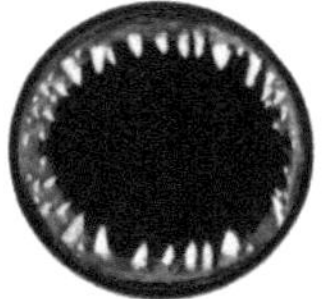

"There is a presence, delivered on the breeze, that only shows itself on Halloween. You feel it in the shiver crawling up your spine and hear it in the rustle of fallen leaves." ~ Lois Fischer

PROLOGUE

Saturday, October 24, 1979

7:30 p.m.

Felix Castillo eased his foot off the gas pedal, bringing the Con Edison utility truck to a stop at the quiet intersection. He proceeded left onto Mountain Avenue, entering the wooded residential development, and made his way towards the dead-end cul-de-sac of Foothills Drive. Sycamores and maples lined the quiet street, most of their leaves already turned deep shades of orange and rust from the seasonably crisp autumn temperatures. Lumbering along at a snail's pace, the electrician checked himself in the rearview and did a double take. The grinning face staring back at him was almost unrecognizable. It'd been a long time since Felix had anything to smile about, and its presence felt out of place. It wasn't like he was depressed or any sadder than the next guy, he just wasn't happy, and his awareness of the malady had grown more acute over the past few months.

Most of the men who worked for Con Edison were already married or had steady girlfriends, of which Felix had neither. A good number of them had children, something Felix was sure he did not want ... until recently, maybe. Having bounced around the foster care system as a child, Felix had always longed to be a part of a family, a real family, one he could call his own. But he'd never been able to connect with a woman on a deep enough level, emotionally or physically. And Felix Castillo had come to accept the idea that that ship had sailed. Up until a few weeks ago, that is. A recent development in his life had changed the way Felix thought about a lot of things ... a development named Mandy Griggs. Felix laughed as he scanned the rearview a second time, ran a hand through his thick, black hair, and allowed his smile to widen until it filled his entire face.

Glowing eyes burned orange against a darkened backdrop of night; carved-out jack-o'-lanterns sat on almost every porch, staring back at Felix as he passed. Plastic skeletons and stuffed bedsheet ghosts hung from tree limbs, swaying like pendulums in the cool October breeze. Felix slowed the truck even further with his face pressed to the window, admiring the yard decorations. The town of Garrett Grove sure did Halloween right. Nearly every front lawn was done up, with each house trying to outdo the next. And with the big night only a week away, it looked like every kid in the Grove would be coming home with a pillowcase full of candy.

Felix turned the truck around at the end of the cul-de-sac and backed in beneath a canopy of overhanging pines. Foothills Drive was his favorite place to park, with only four houses on the entire block, all set far back from the road. The perfect spot to catch an hour or two of uninterrupted shut-eye. As a lineman for the electric company, he preferred the night shift and took all the overtime he could get. Most nights were quiet, with the occasional fried squirrel on a transformer or a fallen tree limb over a power line. Storm season was a different story; from late November through early March, Felix could count on no less than thirty extra hours a week. But tonight, there wasn't much going on in his corner of the world, which consisted of Warren, Parker Plains, and Garrett Grove. And from where he sat beneath the shadow of Garrett Mountain, all was quiet, as if the world had gone to sleep.

Turning off the engine, he listened to the low hum of static from the dispatch radio. The volume was set just loud enough to wake him if he were called. He fumbled for his pack of smokes, rolled down the window, and lit a Marlboro Red. The blazing glow of the Ford's cigarette lighter illuminated the entire cab of the truck.

Felix drew on his smoke and scanned the sports section of the paper. Oct. 24, 1979, **Billy Martin Punches Marshmallow Salesmen, Puts Job in Jeopardy**.

"At it again, huh, Billy?" he said, putting the paper to the side. He yawned and leaned against the seat, allowing thoughts of Mandy to fill his head once again. A vision of the girl in her waitress uniform caused his smile to return, although it was a bit more wicked than the previous one he had worn.

Mandy Griggs worked the morning shift at Wilson's Diner on Route 3. She'd been flirting with Felix for the past month now, but he'd been afraid to make a move. Still, he loved the way her skirt hitched up when she stood on her tiptoes to grab the peach cobbler from the top shelf of the display case.

"You sure do like this peach cobbler," she had teased.

In truth, the cobbler tasted like shit, but it was the only pie on the top shelf. And Felix enjoyed watching Mandy reach for it—so much so, he had packed on a few pounds as a result.

He had a good idea Mandy had moved the pie up there on purpose. She'd been extra flirtatious lately, had started to wear just a little more makeup, and the top button of her blouse seemed to drop one each day—which had been unbuttoned dangerously low to begin with for a family restaurant. As if it had been delivered with a sledgehammer, Felix finally got the message and asked Mandy out. He took her to the Warren Drive-in to see the movie about the haunted house on Long Island and was thrilled to learn that Mandy's blouse could be unbuttoned a hell of a lot more in private.

He couldn't wait to see her again. Strawberry blonde hair and blue eyes, the girl had everything, including a great rack. Felix shifted in his seat, getting excited just thinking about her. *I wonder if she's free tomorrow night—I could go for a double feature.*

He took one last drag from his smoke and pitched the butt out the window. A light garble of static from the radio broke the silence but only for a moment. All was quiet. With the cool air waltzing in against his skin, Felix stretched out and shut his eyes. He thought more about Mandy, happy he had finally asked her out, even happier he could stop eating all that God-awful peach cobbler. Now he didn't need an excuse to get her to hike up her skirt.

The breeze picked up, sending a cold chill racing through the cab of the Ford. It was followed by a scraping sound, as if someone had skidded across the pavement just outside the truck. Felix straightened in his seat and turned toward the street. He reached to roll up the window and hesitated, listening for the furtive sound to return. His heart rate escalated as possible scenarios played out in his head, each one more outrageous than the previous. *What the fuck was that?*

The scuffing could have been caused by an animal, but Felix doubted it had been made by a small one. There were mountain lions and deer living in the woods behind the small development, more than a few bears as well. It was also the week before Halloween, and the idea that someone was hiding in the dark, intent on messing with him, presented itself as a valid possibility. He waited for what felt like an hour, listening, his senses agitated to high alert. He started again as a rattling of dried leaves skirted across the cul-de-sac, carried along by the sudden breeze. Felix watched them tumble over the asphalt and shook his head in relief. "Get a grip, man," he said, realizing he was jumping at shadows.

He smiled once again, but the feature twisted as a frigid rush of air blasted him in the face, silencing his breath like a noose. Felix tried to focus on the wave of distortion before him. He blinked and opened his eyes in time to see it reach for him. It latched onto either side of his skull and yanked him forward. Titanic pressure flooded his brain and bore into him with a vice-like urgency. Every muscle in his body spasmed as if he'd been hit with a cattle prod. He struggled to free himself, but the force was gargantuan. Before he could scream, Felix was ripped out of the driver's side window, breaking four fingers as he fought to hold on to the steering wheel.

Felix didn't know he was airborne until he landed. He came down in the middle of the street with his shoulder shattering on impact. The scream rising in his throat stagnated and never left. The unseen force was on top of him in a heartbeat, biting with the velocity of a chainsaw. He attempted to focus on his assailant, but his vision was obscured by a swirling cloud of darkness. The stench of cold copper invaded his sinuses and filled his lungs. Fighting to speak, Felix lay on his back staring up at a desperate

October sky. A vision of Mandy found its way back as the beast forced itself inside and violated him. It was cold at first but quickly escalated with the intensity of frostbite, then his blood boiled over like hellfire. The night crept in, fading to a toxic grey as Felix was drained. His last thoughts were of Mandy leaning over the counter, her blouse unbuttoned dangerously low. Felix smiled and slipped away with the God-awful taste of peach cobbler lingering on his tongue.

CHAPTER 1

Meanwhile,

Less than a mile away

Lois Fischer sat cross-legged at the large coffee table with the focused attention of ten fourth graders hanging on her every word. She slid the candle towards her and leaned forward, allowing the delicate flame to cast dancing shadows across her face. Meeting the stare of each child for a brief second, Lois paused for dramatic effect. Then she dropped her voice an octave and began to speak.

"There is a presence, delivered on the breeze, that only shows itself on Halloween. You feel it in the shiver crawling up your spine and hear it in the rustle of fallen leaves. A menacing darkness has entered the town, and it knows where you live. It lurks in the shadows, it hides in the woods, waiting for you to take the shortcut through the graveyard. It holds no physical form but watches through the eyes of the jack-o'-lanterns as you make your way home from school. It circles from above, waiting for you to trip and lose your footing. Then it strikes!" Lois raised her voice and slapped her hand against the coffee table, causing a chorus of gasps to erupt from the entranced group of children. She paused once again, then continued.

"Like a raven seizing a shrew. You fight to breathe as you struggle to escape its grip. But it's too late. You succumb to its gravity, paralyzed with fear, and may never know the beast by name ... for it has many names. And it's older than time itself. Only then will you understand what has been delivered on the breeze. Only then will you know the beast by name. You say it with your dying breath ... Ojanox."

"Ow-jo-knocks!" Troy Fischer cried, zeroing in on his mother's sapphire-blue eyes, his own nearly the identical shade.

"No, honey," Lois said, leaning over and ruffling her son's overgrown mop of hair. "It's pronounced, Oh-Zja-Nox."

"Well, that's not scary. Whoever heard of an Ojanox?"

Lois shrugged and returned the candle to the center of the table, illuminating the faces of the ten boys and girls dressed in their Halloween costumes. Beyond the swath of candlelight, the Fischers' living room looked like a scene ripped from the pages of a Bram Stoker novel. Fake cobwebs covered every surface, from the olive-colored love seat to the Pioneer stereo. Half-concealed plastic spiders lurked from their perches, ready to pounce. Glow-in-the-dark skeletons stood in the far corners of the room, and rubber bats hung suction cupped to the windows and the front of the RCA color television set.

Halloween was Troy Fischer's favorite holiday, and it showed. Of course, he loved the candy, but there was more to it than that. It had something to do with what his mother described in her ghost story, although he thought the name of the monster was somewhat silly. There was a strange sense of ominous wonder in the air this time of year, a feeling of tension and mystery that Troy associated with Halloween. This year had brought an added element of excitement with the coming of Troy's second annual Halloween party. This was the first time that Wendy Sirocka was able to attend. The girl had moved to town just last month. Troy also had a special surprise waiting in the garage for his guests ... one that was guaranteed to make them scream.

"I thought it was scary," said Kelly Rainey, who wore a Raggedy Ann costume and sat so close to her friend Caroline Smith, she was almost on top of her. "What about you?" she asked her friend.

"Really scary." Caroline nodded in agreement, the baggy fabric of her Raggedy Andy costume flopping in time.

"Yeah, that was a good one, Mrs. F." Mike Barnes wore a cowboy costume and sat next to his neighbor, Jeff Campbell, who came dressed as Captain Kirk.

"I don't know, Mrs. Fischer," Tommy Negal said. "I don't scare too easy, but it was pretty good."

Troy examined the boy's thrown together hobo outfit and concluded that Tommy had put zero thought into his costume and come up with it at the last minute. Fixing his Dracula fangs for possibly the tenth time in the past five minutes, Troy bared his teeth and checked out the rest of his friends' costumes. Beth Dorn and Terry Wallen both dressed like babies in footy pajamas. And Scott Cole had come as Frankenstein, complete with neck bolts and head piece, and was looking like the clear winner for best costume.

Although *Star Wars* had been out for just over two years and was still all the rage, none of the boys had dressed as Luke Skywalker, Han Solo, or even Darth Vader. The only guest to arrive as a character from the movie was Wendy, who wore a Princess Leia costume. With her long black hair set into tight buns against the sides of her head, the young Italian girl looked exactly like the *Star Wars* heroine. Troy turned to her, feeling the strange fluttering inside his chest once again, and wished he had dressed as Luke Skywalker and not a stupid vampire.

"What did you think?" Troy asked with a tremble in his voice. "Um, about the ghost story, I mean."

"I liked it." Wendy looked back at him, her big chestnut-colored eyes catching him like a deer in the headlights.

Troy coughed, almost swallowed his Dracula fangs, and quickly turned away.

"Who's ready for some cupcakes?" Lois asked, rising to her feet.

"Aw, Mom," Troy said. "It's time for Scream in the Dark."

"I think your friends would like some cupcakes first," she said, making her way to the kitchen and turning on the lights. "Then you can have your haunted house."

Shouts in favor of cupcakes told Troy he was outnumbered. He let out a theatrical sigh, then thought it might be better to scare his friends once they had full stomachs. *Tommy will probably puke.* Troy laughed, but his smile faded as thoughts of Robert Boyle came to mind. Rob was his best friend, had been since their first day of kindergarten. The two boys had worked most of the past week constructing Scream in the Dark, using cardboard they had liberated from the dumpster behind Marcos Playmart to fabricate the labyrinth walls. The boys had originally intended to operate the entire show themselves with the help of Troy's older cousins, Eric and Billy Tobin, who were secretly waiting for the festivities to commence.

Troy and Rob had worked out all the scares and gimmicks on their own, and each had a vital role to play in the night's production. Then Rob had gotten sick at the last minute and been unable to come to the party. To make matters worse, there were others who couldn't be there as well. Both Ben and Erin Richards, the only twins in Troy's class, had also missed school on Friday due to an illness. Whatever Rob had appeared to be going around. But the absence that Troy felt the most, even more than that of his best friend, was his father. Don Fischer had missed a lot of family dinners lately and not been home to help the boys with their construction. And even though he had said, "I wouldn't miss it for the world, kiddo," when Troy asked if he would be home in time for the party, he still hadn't come home from work.

Troy looked up to the wall clock, noticing it was almost eight, then turned his stare to the family portrait hanging next to it. A picture of his mom, dad, and himself, taken a little more than a year ago, smiled back at him and caused him to smile himself. As his friends gravitated to the kitchen to retrieve their cupcakes and juices, Troy's mind wandered to just a few days before when Scream in the Dark was still in its early design stages.

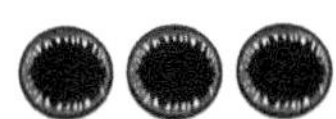

Troy and Rob had begun constructing the haunted house Wednesday after school. They continued their work on Thursday, but there was still much to be done, and they knew they'd be lucky if they finished in time for the party. It had started to get late, and Rob said he had to be home by five-thirty for dinner. So, the boys made plans to finish the following day, and Rob set out for home on his bicycle. His house wasn't far, just under a mile if you stuck to the town's paved roads. Which was something the boys rarely did; the paths through the foothills were the perfect shortcut and their preferred route of transit. A network of trails snaked through the undeveloped woods of King County, separating Mountain Avenue from Foothills Drive, then continued up the north side of Garrett Mountain.

Miss Davis, the third-grade teacher, had taken Troy's class there on a field trip last year. She told them how the Lenni Lenape tribe had lived in the area for centuries and that the paths through the foothills were old game trails used for hunting. Scott Cole had even found an arrowhead, which sparked a treasure hunting frenzy in the entire class. After that, Rob and Troy returned to the foothills every chance they could; arrowhead fever was at an all-time high.

After Rob had left, Troy continued to plug away in the garage until he was called into the house. He was handed the phone to find Rob's mother on the line. "Troy, this is Mrs. Boyle. Robert isn't home yet," she said. "Is he still there?"

"Um, n-no," Troy said. "He left, like, an hour ago. But I wouldn't worry; he must've stopped to look for arrowheads on the trail." He cleared his throat, then told her how Rob would probably be home any minute. Which is exactly what happened, and Rob walked through the front door while Troy was still on the line.

"Thank you, Troy," Mrs. Boyle said. "Rob will call you later, if he can still walk after the beating he's about to get. But it's not looking good."

When Rob didn't show up for school the next day, Troy figured Mrs. Boyle had kept good on her word and given him a good licking. He called his friend as soon as he got home, only Mrs. Boyle answered.

"I'm sorry, Troy. Robert's sick and can't come to the phone." She said it was probably the flu and doubted if Rob would be able to make it to the Halloween party.

Troy had felt his chest deflate as if all his ten-year-old dreams had been crushed with one fell swoop. It was devastating that Rob might not make it to the party; even worse, they had planned to go trick-or-treating together, and Halloween was only a week away.

25

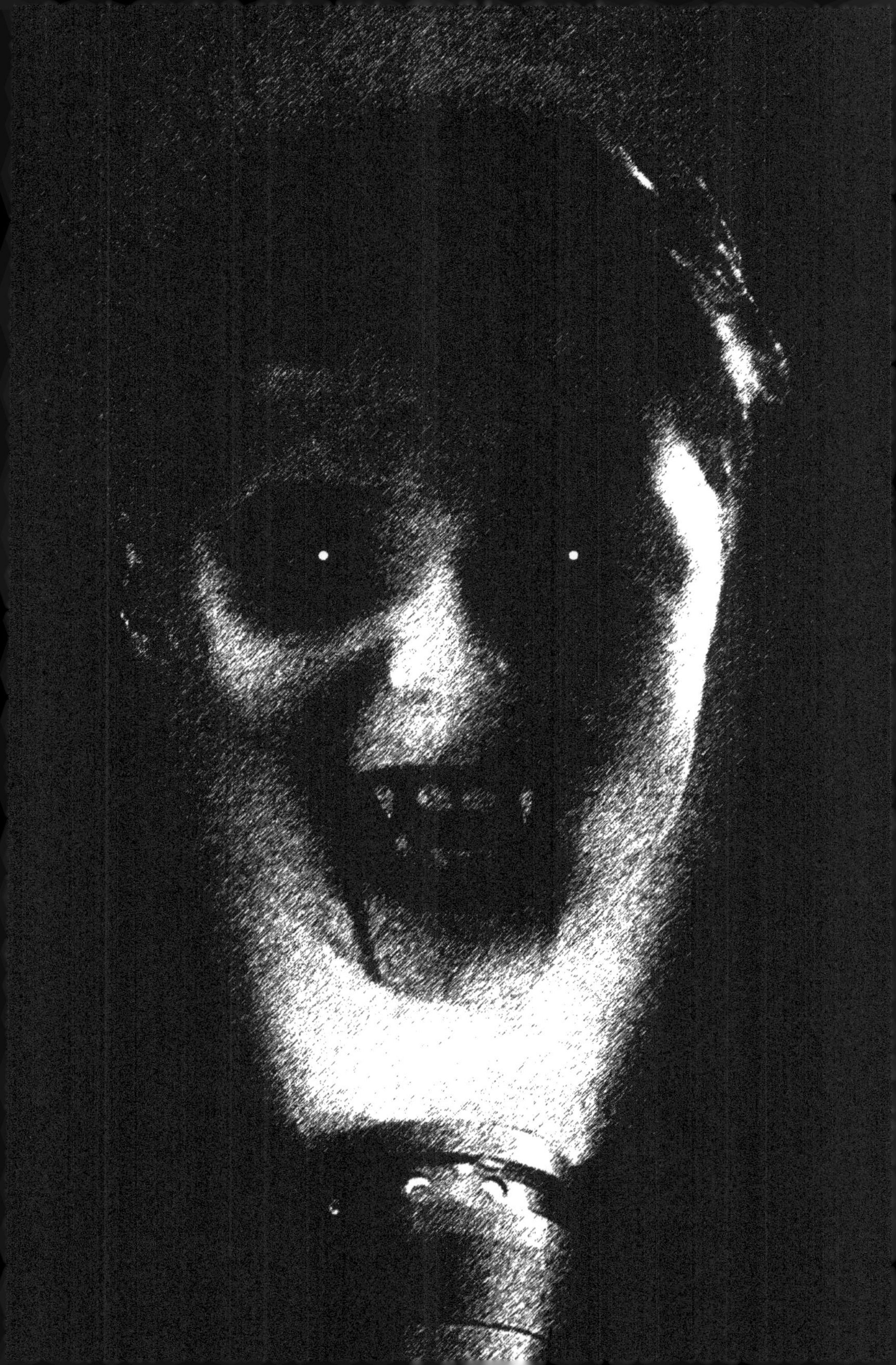

CHAPTER 2

After the cupcakes were devoured, the children walked single file out the front door, into the cool, crisp night. Candles had been set along the walkway leading from the porch to the Fischers' garage. Troy guided his friends with a flashlight held beneath his chin; Wendy followed a close step behind, bumping into him every time he stopped to speak.

"I warn you, what you are about to see may give you nightmares," Troy said, trying to sound like Bella Lugosi. "There are things inside that want to eat you!" He shouted the last two words, causing Wendy and several of the other girls to scream.

"Come on, let's go, Count Dorkula," Mike said, inciting a fresh fit of laughter.

"Follow me then ... if you dare."

The front of the garage had been blocked off with thick sheets of cardboard painted black. Troy led the children to the right, through a makeshift door, and ushered them into the darkness. Once the last child was inside, the door slammed shut behind them and Troy stopped short to block their path. The walls of the narrow hallway were tight on either side, with no room for the children to turn around. Suffocating night closed in around them, making it impossible to see. Cries of discomfort and confusion started much sooner than Troy had anticipated. He continued to hold his ground and remained silent, allowing their disorientation to escalate. But the total darkness and claustrophobia proved too much for his friends, and they started to panic.

"What's going on?" Beth cried out. The sound of hands slapping against the cardboard walls of the hallways echoed throughout.

"I can't see anything. Stop touching me!" Terry yelled. There was a folly of grunts and groans as the tangle of children pressed against one another.

"Hey!" someone else screamed.

Troy stifled his laughter and pictured what was about to happen.

"This is stu—" Mike's voice was silenced as the tiny hallway exploded with a flurry of sound and vision. The blinding pulse of a strobe light and the ear-piercing blare of tortured screams assaulted the children like mortar fire. Arms reached for them, clawing and grabbing, materializing from the very walls themselves. Unknown to the children, they had been standing inches away from the window of a cage. The Tobin brothers howled like wild animals from behind the bars that covered the opening. Both wore werewolf masks and clawed at Troy's friends, who were now screaming and desperate to get away from their attackers.

Troy held his ground, refusing to budge; there was nowhere for the trapped children to go as his cousins played their part to the fullest. One of the kids had started to cry, and Troy was pretty sure it was Tommy. *Oh boy, here comes the puke.*

The strobe had disorientated everyone as planned, and the screams played through the giant boom box had come on at the perfect moment. Troy jumped as something brushed up against him and took his hand.

It had been Wendy. The strange fluttering returned, causing his heart to pound so hard he felt it in his throat. Sweat started to slick his brow, and for a moment, Troy forgot where he was. The sight of his cousins in their wolf masks snapped him back to the moment. He returned the flashlight to his chin and shouted to be heard over the noise.

"Quick, follow me ... this way." He pulled Wendy by the hand and led everyone through the door behind him.

The next hallway was covered in webs. Two black lights mounted to the ceiling illuminated the glow-in-the-dark spiders that began to descend upon them.

"Don't let them touch you. They are highly venomous! One bite, and you are a goner!"

The children followed him out of the room as the arachnids continued to drop on them. Troy was pretty sure he had scared the daylights out of everyone and figured he'd move them along to the next big scare.

He stopped at the next door. "I don't know what's in here, but it doesn't sound good." The squealing sounds of rodents filled their ears. "I hope you're not afraid of rats!" he shouted over the din.

They entered a room even darker than the first, making it impossible for the children to see the rubber hoses lining the floor. Billy, Troy's oldest cousin, operated the mechanism controlling the rat hoses from the safety of his hiding place on the other side of the wall. The shrieking cries of vermin pumped through the hidden stereo speakers was deafening.

"Oh my God! I stepped on something!" Caroline screamed.

"They're everywhere!" someone shouted.

The further they walked into the room, the deeper the carpet of hoses grew, making it feel as if rats were being crushed under their feet. Troy felt his smile threaten to take his entire face as he noticed how lifelike the sensation of the rats really felt.

"One's in my hair! Get it out!"

Troy squeezed Wendy's hand and pressed forward, leading his friends out of the rat menagerie and through another doorway. They entered a room longer and wider than the others, which took up nearly one third of the entire garage. A deep crimson glow bathed the room in a blood-like wash as organ music, piped in from some unseen source, provided the demonic soundtrack.

"This can't be good," Troy said, leading them further inside.

The room before them revealed itself to be a graveyard. Headstones were set with names written on them: I.P. Daily on one and Bob Frapples on another. A small fence separated the children from the far side of the room, where a large coffin sat propped against the wall.

"I better check this out." Wendy tried to hold onto his hand as Troy pulled away. "Don't worry, I'll be right back." He popped the small capsule into his mouth without anyone noticing and stepped over the fence.

The other children held their breath and watched Troy approach the coffin. His cape hung inches from the floor as he walked through the graveyard and knelt beside the casket. "That's what I thought," he gasped.

Eric Tobin lay inside the coffin waiting for his cue, and that was it. He bolted upright and seized Troy by the shoulders, pulling him toward the sarcophagus. Troy screamed and bit down on the capsule.

The boys struggled for a moment as Eric pretended to sink his fangs into Troy's neck before releasing him. Troy fell backwards toward the fence. Blood dripped from his mouth as he looked up at his friends and screamed. "Get out! While you still can!" He collapsed on the floor. A second later, Eric started to rise from the coffin.

The children jumped back into the wall behind them and clamored about to find an exit. They pounded against the cardboard, which appeared as sturdy as brick and refused to budge. They tried every surface but couldn't find a way out. Kelly and Caroline screamed as several of the kids knocked into them. The sound of one boy crying was distinct above the insanity of noises.

"I think I found it!" Wendy shouted and pressed up against what she thought was the exit. The others followed, jamming the little girl against the wall. Together, they clawed at the slit that had to be the doorway.

Eric emerged from the coffin and stepped over the fence. He raised his arms towards the frightened children and moaned.

"Why isn't it opening?" Kelly whined.

"Push harder," Tommy cried, ready to puke.

"Stop it. You're crushing me," Wendy shouted.

With a sudden rush, the door flew open, and the mass of boys and girls tumbled out onto the Fischers' driveway, safe and unharmed. The cool October air vaporized their breath, revealing it in exaggerated plumes of condensation.

"Oh my God! That was so scary," Caroline gasped.

"Cool," Jeff agreed.

Troy and his cousins scrambled out the back entrance of the garage and listened to the conversations from their hiding place.

"That wasn't scary. It was pretty dumb, if you ask me," Mike said, leaning against the side of the house.

It was the exact cue Troy had been hoping to hear. He gave his cousins the okay signal and the boys broke cover, jumping out of the darkness from the side of the garage, screaming and grabbing at the other children. Eric and Billy had donned their masks and tore after Mike and Tommy, who ran from the driveway with the werewolves in hot pursuit. The rest of the group scattered for a moment, then regrouped and started to laugh. Troy joined them, with his smile growing wider by the second. Every trick and gimmick had worked like a charm, just as he and Rob had planned.

"You scared me half to death." Wendy approached Troy and punched him in the arm.

The other kids chimed in, voicing their approval as well. Jeff patted him on the back, Scott and Caroline told him what rooms they liked best, while Terry and Beth continued to hug each other, attempting to steady their nerves. The sound of Mike and Tommy screaming in the distance helped everyone shake off the fright Troy had given them. A few moments later, they were all giggling and laughing it up.

"How did everything go?" Lois asked as she entered the driveway.

"Great," Troy said with a ribbon of fake blood clinging to his chin.

"Was it a graveyard smash?"

"Mom!" Troy rolled his eyes and shook his head.

"Well, I thought it was funny," she said. "There's some pizza left if anyone's still hungry." Lois turned and headed back into the house, and the other children followed, leaving Wendy and Troy alone in the driveway.

"You really liked it?" Troy asked. "Scream in the Dark?"

"It was awesome. Could you show me again?"

"Well, it won't be the same without Eric and Billy working the lights and stuff." Troy couldn't think of a reason why she might want to see it again. *It won't even be scary now that you know what happens.* But Wendy insisted.

"That's okay. I just want you to show me."

"Well okay. Follow me then." He opened the first door, revealing the hallway with the cage set in the center of the wall. The strobe light still flashed at a tantric pace, making Troy feel lightheaded as he led Wendy by the hand. Then she stopped, tugged on his arm, and pulled him back. Troy turned around, but before he could react, Wendy kissed him. It was quick and awkward as her lips pecked him half on his bottom lip and half on his chin. Troy felt the blood rush to his face and the sensation of pins and needles dancing over every inch of his skin. A lump the size of a softball formed in his throat as the narrow hallway tilted to the left and threatened to knock him off his feet. He had been blindsided by her forwardness, having never kissed or been kissed by a girl before. Wendy stepped back, bit her lip, and smiled.

"Umm," Troy managed.

"I like you, Troy," she said.

"Umm, you do?"

"Yes ... do you like me?"

"Umm ... yes." The ability to speak slipped further from his grasp.

Wendy took a step forward and kissed him again. He was a bit more prepared this time and managed to pucker his lips and offer a feeble kiss back. It was a gallant effort for the ten-year-old boy.

But the moment was brought to an abrupt halt when Billy and Eric chased Mike and Tommy back into the driveway. The four boys huddled outside the door as Troy and Wendy nervously exited the garage. The guilty-as-sin look they both wore was unseen by the other children. But when they entered the house, it was noticed immediately.

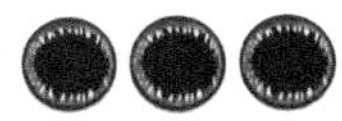

Call it mother's intuition. Lois Fischer watched her son and his new friend as they took their pizza and retreated to the living room, away from the other kids. The forty-five of the Monster Mash spun on the turntable for the umpteenth time in a row, and the hyper banter of the ten fourth graders made Lois's head swim. From what she could make out of the conversations, Scream in the Dark had been a total success. A satisfied grin lit her face as she entered the living room to offer Troy and Wendy a refill of juice, and to conduct a little snooping as well.

"More Kool Aid?" She approached with a pitcher.

"No thanks, Mom." Troy fidgeted in his seat, shifting his gaze to the floor.

"No, thank you, Mrs. Fischer," the little Italian girl said with a blush.

"Did you have a nice time, Wendy?" Lois asked, her smirk growing wider by the second.

"Yes."

Troy continued to squirm as if his underwear was too tight.

Lois tried her best to stifle her laughter at the sight of her son. The kid was a mess compared to Wendy, who played it as cool as a snow cone. *This one is going to be a handful.* Allowing a devious smile to slip, she started to head toward the kitchen, then turned back. "Oh, Wendy," she said.

"Yes, Mrs. Fischer?"

"You've got something on your chin." Lois dropped the bomb, then waited at the entrance to the kitchen to witness the reaction.

Wendy rubbed her hand against her face and came away with a red smear on her palm. Lois watched as the child's face flushed crimson like the fake blood on her chin, a near identical match to the color and location of the stain that Troy wore. Wendy's jaw dropped as she stared down at the stain. She quickly looked up at Lois, then back at her hand, and finally turned to Troy, who still had no idea his mom had figured everything out in less than two minutes. But Lois could see the realization in Wendy eyes; the girl knew she'd been caught and darted from her chair and ran toward the bathroom. *Girls really do mature quicker than boys.*

Wendy left Troy in a huff, racing past Billy and Eric Tobin just as they entered the room.

"That was radical," Billy said to his younger cousin, shoving the last bite of pizza into his mouth. "To be honest, I thought it was gonna be dumb, but you really pulled it off. Can't wait till next year."

"Did you see their faces when we jumped 'em?" Eric asked, still wearing his werewolf mask. "I thought the one kid was gonna piss himself ... he might have."

"You guys were great," Troy said, looking up at his cousins. Billy and Eric could have almost passed for twins if Billy wasn't six inches taller than his younger brother. With their sandy-brown hair and sapphire-blue eyes, they looked like nearly grown versions of Troy, and resembled Lois as well. "The graveyard was awesome. They were stuck, just like we planned."

"Piece of cake," Billy said. "No way I was letting them out."

Billy had barricaded the door from the other side, using a board of sheet rock and his own teenage strength.

"Right on!" Troy said, trying to sound cool to the older boys.

"Whatever, dork!" Billy laughed and punched his younger cousin in the arm. Although it had been a friendly blow, it stung just the same. Troy did his best not to show it. The three boys looked up as Wendy returned to the living room with no sign of the incriminating smear on her chin. Troy's entire body went rigid as she walked across the shag carpet towards him. Billy examined his actions and threw him a wink. "Well, kiddo," he said, clapping Troy on the back. "We gotta scram. Big night, if you know what I mean."

"Um ... not really." Troy shrugged his shoulders, clueless to Billy's suggestion.

"Well," Billy said, raising his eyebrows as Wendy passed him. "Give it a couple years and you will. Oh, and I get to be the vampire next Halloween."

"I got something even scarier planned for next year."

"I don't know about that, kiddo. You really outdid yourself. Well, see ya later, squirt."

"Where are you boys off to?" Lois popped her head out of the kitchen.

"You know, big date, Aunt Lois." Billy offered an exaggerated wink. "Can't keep the ladies waiting."

"Hmm-mmm." She smirked. "Well, be careful driving. I know there won't be any drinking involved, right?"

"We're not old enough to drink, Aunt Lois," Eric said, lifting his mask to kiss her on the cheek.

"See you soon." Billy kissed her as well, and the Tobin brothers exited out the front door. Eric replaced his mask and howled all the way to the car.

"Is your mother picking you up, Wendy?" Lois asked.

"Yes, Mrs. Fischer. She should be here any minute now," Wendy said politely. "Thank you for having me." Wendy's mother and father were divorced, and her dad lived in Warren. And although her mom had tried to fill Wendy's head with cautionary tales of how horrible men were, Wendy had a willful mind of her own. Sometimes a bit too willful for her own good.

Troy thanked his friends, who agreed it had been a radical haunted house and a groovy party. Then, one by one, the children's parents arrived in their Pintos and Toyotas, honking their horns to announce their arrival.

When Wendy's mother showed up, Troy walked her to the door and opened it.

"That was a cool haunted house, Troy." She bit her lip again.

"I'm glad you liked it. I hope it wasn't too scary," he said, feeling the confidence swell within him.

Lois listened from the kitchen while Troy exercised his newfound bravado.

"I was okay." Wendy stepped onto the front porch, hesitated, then doubled back. "Because you were there." She stuck her head in the doorway and pecked him on the cheek. "See you Monday at school." She darted off the steps, raced across the lawn, and jumped into the backseat of her mother's station wagon.

Troy watched her leave, then shut the door. He turned to find his mother, Scott, Kelly, and Caroline staring at him with giant grins plastered to their faces.

"Troy's got a girlfriend," Caroline snickered.

"Troy and Wendy, sitting in a tree," Kelly ribbed.

Before Scott could add a clever comment of his own, the fortunate sound of a car horn broke the tension. Kelly's mom had arrived to drive the three of them home. They ran down the stairs as if on cue, shouting, "Thanks, Mrs. Fischer, great party. See ya Monday."

Troy had been spared ... almost.

His mom continued to grin at him from her perch at the top of the stairs.

"What?!" he blurted.

"I didn't say anything." She walked back to the kitchen and added, "Think you can help your mother clean up, Romeo?"

"Aw, Mom!" Troy let out an exasperated sigh, shook his head, and followed her into the kitchen.

CHAPTER 3

Mountainside Park sat at the top of Mountain Avenue and wasn't much more than a glorified dirt parking lot at the end of a dead-end road—but the view was spectacular. Here, one could see the entire town of Garrett Grove, from the steeple of the Lutheran church, all the way to the banks of the Lenape River, and everything in between. Mountain Avenue—known to the locals as Mountain Ave—sat on the north side of town, originating at the base of the foothills. Then it took a steep climb up the side of Garrett Mountain, where it dead-ended at the park. It was a favorite spot for family picnics on Sunday afternoons and teenage make-out sessions on Friday and Saturday nights.

But to call Mountain Ave a dead-end wasn't entirely accurate. Although the road was closed where the park had been established, the old extension continued well past the barricade and snaked up the mountain a good mile and a half further.

The weed-strewn, pothole-filled old extension, which had been closed for decades, corkscrewed and twisted up the mountain like a crooked politician. This treacherous piece of blacktop led to the Mountainside Sanatorium, which sat vacant at the summit in a state of rot and decay. The sanatorium had been built in 1890 to house consumption patients. As tuberculosis spread like wildfire during the 19th century, sanatoriums in isolated locations began to pop up across the country, the idea being that contagious patients would greatly benefit from the open setting and spacious properties. These facilities promised a certain level of accommodation to those who could afford them. However, Mountainside was anything but a place of comfort and grace.

As the disease had reached pandemic proportions, the sanatoriums were forced to open their doors to the public. This led to an indigestible level of suffering. Patients were left to waste in overcrowded sick rooms as TB stole their breath. There was no cure, and there was no relief. There was only pain and desolation. Finally, the first consumption patient was cured in 1949 with a drug called Streptomycin. Mountainside Sanatorium closed its doors in 1952, but not before the stain of despair saturated the ground. The building had been left standing there ever since.

The copper wiring and light fixtures had been stripped by scrappers looking to make a few extra bucks. Most of the windows were shattered, and nature crept in through every possible crevice. Graffiti covered most of the walls, and beer cans and cigarette butts littered the floors. But other than that, the place was intact.

The sanatorium looked as if it had been abandoned in a hurry. Gurneys and beds still occupied the rooms and halls, files were left in cabinets, and furniture still sat in the doctors' offices. It was like the place closed overnight, as if the staff had made a run for it.

Now there were more rumors about the sanatorium than facts. It had become such a sour piece of the town's history that most people pretended it never existed at all. So it sat at the top of Garrett Mountain in a state of disrepair, growing more mysterious with each passing year. The only visitors were the occasional vagrants, and teenagers looking for a place to drink and make out. Since Garrett Grove didn't have much of a vagrant problem, and the old road was lined with potholes large enough to swallow a small child, the place didn't get many visitors. However, there was nothing more determined than horny teenagers looking for a place to screw.

The six high school students stood in the abandoned parking lot beneath a blanket of stars, staring at the ominous structure. The place was enormous and loomed before them in the darkness like a monolith. Several buildings jutted out from the main structure, and smaller houses called "the cottages" peppered the outskirts of the property. That was where the hospital staff had lived.

"There's no way I'm going in there," Debbie Horne said. Her straight, dark hair hung to the small of her back, resembling the pop singer Crystal Gayle, or so she liked to think. Unfortunately, thinking she looked like Crystal Gayle didn't make Debbie's brown eyes any bluer and it didn't make her look anything like Crystal Gayle, but she was still pretty enough for Billy Tobin. "You couldn't pay me to step one foot in that place."

"What?" Billy cried. "After we walked up the whole damn mountain, you're gonna chicken out on me?" He wrapped his arms around her and groped just a little. "I'm not gonna let anybody get you, baby. I promise."

"Stop it, you pig," she said, halfheartedly fending him off.

Eric Tobin let out a howl, still wearing the werewolf mask from the party. "Oww." He panted and pretended to bite Susan Smith on the neck. She pulled his mask off and kissed him on the lips.

"Easy, boy," she said. "You don't have to beg."

Susan was Caroline Smith's older sister, which was obvious. Both girls wore the same blonde curls and revealed identical dimples when they smiled. Susan and Eric had been dating since their freshman year, and this wasn't her first visit to the sanatorium, but she could remember how freaked out she had been. She knew exactly what Debbie was feeling, being her first time and all. Also, Debbie and Billy had been dating for less than a month.

"Anybody want a beer?" Mick Petrie asked. He had known Billy and Eric for years and gotten into nearly as much trouble as the two brothers. Mick was the jock of the group, and even though he was stronger and faster than his friends, he still followed Billy Tobin around like a faithful servant. He and his girlfriend, Allison Aigans, had been to the old sanatorium more than a few times before.

"Oh yeah." Billy grabbed a can for him and one for Debbie. "So, what do you want to do, stand here in the dark all night?"

"No," Debbie said, opening her beer. "I guess not."

A crescent moon shined down and blanketed the massive complex in a silvery-blue light. Shadows jumped from the overgrown scrub grass that wove its way between the cracks in the pavement. The structure, a sour face at the top of a haggard body, kept a silent watch, an imposing sil-houette against a backdrop of night. Billy cast the beam of his flashlight across the front façade of the old hospital, revealing paint that had peeled away to nothing and loose brickwork that had broken free. Not even the vines creeping up the front of the building were able to hold it together. Eventually, the entire place would crumble to the ground. The light caught a family of raccoons as they scurried across the front steps.

"What the hell is that?" Allison ran behind Mick and latched onto him, her skin-tight corduroy slacks swooshing as her thighs rubbed against one other.

"Maybe it's the knob goblins," Mick answered. "I hear they feast on virgins—oh wait, you have nothing to worry about."

She slapped him. "Very funny, asshole."

"Well"—Billy pulled Debbie closer—"you don't want the knob goblins to get you. I can make sure they leave you alone and fix that whole virginity thing tonight."

Debbie opened her mouth to reply but stopped when something else darted across the front steps of the building. It was dark and low to the ground, much larger than a raccoon, but there was nothing recognizable about the form. It shot from the left to right like a bullet and was too fast to follow. Billy jumped as it passed through the beam of the light. The others had seen it too and reacted the same.

"What the hell was that?" Mick started.

Debbie screamed and hid behind Billy.

It registered as a blur, moving too quick to even cast a shadow. Billy tried to follow its path with his flashlight but was unsuccessful. He swept the beam to either side of the hospital's main entrance, surveying the grounds, but couldn't find anything.

There was movement behind them, furtive and threatening. It was more like a sensation than an actual sound. Intuition screamed. Something was rapidly approaching from the darkness; the entire group turned as if on cue. Billy cast the light into the murk only to reveal a parking lot of overgrown weeds, empty and deserted.

"I don't like this, man." Eric's voice was little more than a whisper. "We should get out of here."

For a moment, they stood there, breathing heavily into the cool night. Silence fell like a blanket; even the crickets were hushed, as if they had been erased from existence. Something just beyond the reach of the light waited. They all felt it. A predator lurking in the shadows. The only sound Billy heard was his heart thrumming in his chest. He nearly screamed when Debbie pulled herself behind him and whispered in his ear. "We need to leave ... Now!"

The others remained still, waiting for Billy to tell them what to do. Instead, he stood there, focusing on the patch of earth just beyond the reach of the light. He could almost see the hazy image—wavering—black against black; it made his eyes hurt to look at it. Whatever was out there had stopped moving.

It was watching them.

The night grew deathly still, and a low-lying ground fog crept in at the edge of their periphery. Billy turned to Debbie and took her hand. "Let's go," he mouthed to the group, just loud enough for them to hear. He started to walk back toward the road but found it impossible to restrain himself from running and tore off in the direction of the old extension as if his head were on fire.

"Come on, let's go!" he screamed to the others.

They didn't need to be told a third time and followed close enough to be on his heels. No one said a word. Fear and panic took root and nearly paralyzed them. If it hadn't been for Billy, they would still be standing in the darkness, exposed and vulnerable.

They descended the steep slope of the extension, being as careful as possible not to break an ankle on the loose asphalt or in any of the numerous potholes. Billy had an overpowering urge to look over his shoulder but didn't dare. He was sure whatever was out there was hunting them. He sensed its pursuit as they made their way further from the old building.

Susan cried out as her feet tangled on a branch in the road. She fell hard to the pavement on her hands and knees. Eric rushed to her side to help as Billy paused to cast the light in their direction. The air above them parted in a flurry of disruption as something passed just inches from their heads. Billy felt his ears pop as the presence descended upon him. It had shot down from the top of the mountain and nearly scalped them. The attack was followed by the scraping sound of loose gravel disturbed in the gloom further down the hill.

Now it was in front of them.

"It's fucking hunting us, Billy!" Eric shouted.

The girls cried as the group huddled close together in the middle of the deserted road. Casting his flashlight in frantic, searching sweeps, Billy prayed nothing would be illuminated; he knew whatever was out there would be unbearable to see.

"What the fuck are we going to do, Billy?" Debbie clung to him, terrified and trembling.

Billy felt close to tears himself and didn't have any answers. He continued to sweep the perimeter with the light, the beam jumping from the tremble of his grip. A strangled cry escaped from his lips when Mick took hold of his shoulder.

"What the hell is that?" Billy's voice shook.

"I don't know, but I have an idea." Mick spoke low and deliberately. "We're gonna count to three. Then I need you to shine the light up the hill, and I'm gonna make a run for it."

"No way, you're not leaving me," Allison protested.

"Don't worry; I'm the fastest one here." Mick had been on the track team since sixth grade and was the fastest kid in school. "I'll head into the woods and then double back. I'll probably get to the car before you do."

"I can't let you do it, man," Billy said.

"You don't have a choice," Mick reassured him, gripping his shoulder. "Three. Two. One." Mick sped off like a bat out of hell, and Billy trained the light up the hill to help guide him.

The sound of scraping gravel echoed below their position. Then the air above them rippled once again, as if a flurry of wings had taken flight. It felt oppressive as it passed overhead and pursued into the night after Mick.

"Come on, quick!" Billy ran, and the others followed.

Their feet skidded and slipped on the loose gravel, but somehow, none of them fell as they barreled down the side of the mountain. Billy yanked at Debbie's arm, pulling her behind him. Eric and Allison flanked Susan to help her along. With every frantic step, they prepared for something to swoop down and carry one of them off into the night.

They crashed into the gate at the bottom of the hill and skirted around it toward the park. Billy let go of Debbie's hand and pulled out his car keys. He unlocked the driver's side, and everyone poured into his Charger through the one open door. Then he jumped in and slammed it shut behind him. Sweat ran down the back of his shirt as he tried to catch his breath. The others stared back at him, wide-eyed and panting. No one spoke.

Billy didn't know what to do. He wanted to go after Mick but was too scared to propose the idea. He put the key into the ignition and sat behind the wheel, waiting for something brilliant to come to him. He was out of ideas.

"We can't just leave him out there." Allison broke the silence. "We have to do something."

"Okay, okay," Billy replied.

"We have to do something, Billy," she cried.

"What the hell do you want me to do?!" he shouted. "If you got any ideas, I'm all ears."

"Easy, bro," Eric said. "Let's just sit here a second and figure this out."

"We can't just sit here. Mick's out there ... he needs our help!" Allison insisted.

Billy felt like jumping into the backseat and strangling the girl but managed to control himself. Before he could reply, the car shook as something heavy landed on the hood. The girls screamed, and Billy turned on the headlights. Perched in front of them, illuminated in the glow, stood Mick, grinning like a clown. He was flushed and out of breath, but he was smiling. He walked around to the passenger side, and Eric let him in.

"You scared the crap out of me," Allison said, pulling him into the backseat. She threw her arms around him and kissed him.

"Ouch." Mick flinched. "That hurts."

"What is it?" Susan asked. "Turn on the lights, Billy."

Billy hit the interior lights and turned to find Mick bleeding from a small wound just below his jaw.

"What happened?" Allison had gotten some blood on her when she grabbed him.

Mick put his hand to his neck to stop the bleeding, which didn't appear too bad. "I ran into a branch or something. It was hard to see, but I think I lost it in the woods. I don't know what the hell's out there, but it sure is fast. Damn thing was right on me too."

Billy started the car, put it in drive, and skidded out of the dirt parking lot. He looked back at Mick in the rearview mirror. "Are you okay, man?"

"Never better." Mick smiled. "Except for one thing."

"What's that?" Eric asked, concerned.

"I dropped the beer." Mick started to laugh, but no one joined him.

The tires chirped as they met the blacktop, with Billy's foot pressed firmly to the floor. He didn't like how pale Mick looked but was happy to put some distance between them and the mountain. He turned on the radio to help lighten the mood, and Buck Dharma's voice filled the cab of the Charger. Billy didn't appreciate the way the singer insisted that he shouldn't fear the reaper, so he turned off the radio and drove in silence.

CHAPTER 4

After all the guests had gone home from the party, Lois watched her son as he absentmindedly tossed paper cups and plates into the trash with a giant grin plastered to his face. "I've never seen anyone so happy to throw out trash," she snickered.

"Huh?" Troy hadn't heard a word.

"Your friends looked like they had a nice time."

"Oh yeah," he said. "It was awesome. You should have seen it, Mom. We scared the heck out of them."

"Umm-hmm, and Wendy looked like she had a nice time."

"Yeah. I mean, I think she did." His face darkened a shade.

"She's pretty. Don't you think?"

"Mom," he pleaded. "Stop it."

"Okay, kiddo. Just don't grow up too fast?" Lois kissed the top of his head.

"Sure, no problem." Troy scanned the kitchen for a diversion to escape from the conversation. "I'm gonna take out the garbage," he said, lifting the bag from the can and heading for the door.

"Thanks, sweetie," she called to him. "Make sure you blow out all the candles."

"Okay, Mom."

"And close up the garage too."

"Got it," he said and walked outside.

Troy threw the garbage into one of the metal cans his father kept on the side of the driveway. Donald Fischer had wanted to be there to help with his son's haunted house but had been unable because of work. Don was a geological engineer for DuCain Industries. The company had been cutting into the mountain on the far side of town for the past decade. Troy had no idea what needed to be done at a quarry on a Saturday night, but his father had said something big happened earlier in the week, that he and a few of the other men would have to burn the midnight oil. Troy had no idea what that meant since DuCain wasn't in the oil business. As far as he knew, they mined minerals and supplied crushed stone for construction. Although, he wasn't exactly sure about that either.

Troy followed the path to the garage, pausing to blow out the candles along the way. He stopped in front of the large overhead door and reached up to grab it. Gripping the handle, he began to pull down. A loud thud, as if something significant had fallen inside, caused Troy to jump. He stood there listening.

All was quiet. He thought maybe the piece of sheet rock Billy had used as a barricade might have fallen over. Then he noticed the strobe light was still flashing and realized he had left the other lights on as well.

Troy entered the strobe-lit hallway and walked past the cage into the spider chamber. He proceeded into the rat menagerie and was gripped by an unshakable sense that he was no longer alone. An icy chill caused the wispy hairs on his arms to prickle; it crept in between his ribs and wrapped around his heart. Despite the rising tension fluttering inside his chest, Troy's legs continued to propel him forward. Step by step, he maneuvered through the darkness and navigated his way across the carpet of rubber hoses. Carefully, he opened the door to the graveyard room and scanned the area, waiting for his eyes to adjust to the dull glow cast from the crimson lightbulbs.

The dimly lit room revealed itself in a wash of scarlet shadows as Troy took another step inside. The fence and the headstones, even the coffin, all appeared as he had last seen them; nothing looked out of place. Troy exhaled and began to turn when a splash of motion caught his attention. A gasp rose in the back of his throat but was silenced, the saliva in his mouth drying up like it had been hit with a blow torch. Behind the coffin against the far wall, the scarlet shadow shifted once again.

Arctic fingers gripped him on either side of his head, then spread downward until the ice water settled in his arms and legs. Unable to move, Troy stood frozen in place with his eyes focused on the dark figure in the corner of the room. The intruder stood facing the far wall with their back to him. Even in the dull amber glow, Troy thought it must be a child, as the figure appeared roughly the same height as he. Not sure if he should call out or turn and run, he stood there trying to grasp a rational explanation. *Is that Tommy ... or Mike?* It was possible his friends had returned to pay him back for scaring them. Troy examined the room to see if anyone else was hiding in the shadows. But he had watched his friends leave when their parents picked them up. He dismissed the notion as he suddenly realized the identity of the figure in the darkness.

"H-Hello," the word cracked from his parched mouth.

The young boy slowly turned toward him. Scarlet shadows danced across his face and revealed his features—it was Rob.

"Rob, what are you doing?" Troy asked.

The child was barefoot and dressed only in his pajamas. Troy noticed his friend's feet right away; they were scraped and cut and covered in dirt. Rob's mouth hung open; his eyes stared back blankly at Troy. Even in the crimson light, his face was visibly ashen and grey, with deep purple streaks on his cheeks and lips.

"Are you okay? What are you doing here?" Troy asked again.

Rob took a step toward him and then another. The boy raised his arms and closed in on Troy.

"Stop playing. You're scaring me."

Rob opened his mouth, allowing a low, guttural hiss to escape. He took another step forward and backed Troy up against the wall. Then Rob lunged at him but suddenly stopped like he had changed his mind at the last second. He looked up at Troy, blinking and confused, as if he were in shock.

"Troy," Rob said in a voice as weak as dust. He scanned the room and then looked down at his bare feet. "Troy, what am I doing here?"

Before Troy could answer, Rob collapsed into his arms. He struggled to hold him, but the boy was as heavy as a sack of wet flour. Troy could feel the heat pouring off his friend's body as he attempted to ease him to the floor. Then Rob's eyes rolled back in their sockets, and he started to convulse.

"Mom!" Troy screamed. "Mom, help! Something's wrong with Rob!"

Donald Fischer and Mark Gold sat at their desks in the large trailer that served as the site supervisor's office. Mark's desk was covered with topographic prints of alternate blast sites. He shifted through the seemingly endless rolls of blue paper with a cigarette suspended from his lips. Smoke lifted into his squinted eyes and rolled over a set of brows so thick, they resembled a pair of Gypsy Moth caterpillars. Donald was on the phone attempting to quell the shitstorm that had blown up in their faces. Early Tuesday morning, routine blasting had revealed a large cavity in a cliff wall on the north face. It was initially thought to be part of an old, abandoned mine, although there were no records indicating the presence of one. Still, it was possible; they came across them from time to time. Which was dangerous as hell due to the pockets of methane they often contained.

It was Don's job to verify safe blast sites. And everything had looked green across the board. Seismic tests hadn't revealed any cavities or abnormalities in the topography. No one was more surprised than he when the smoke cleared and the cave's small opening was revealed.

The markings on the rock near the entrance determined they hadn't uncovered any mine. The ancient symbols resembled hieroglyphs. From what Don could tell, the blast had opened either a burial site or a tribal habitat. Whatever it was, it was old as hell and would prove to be one giant pain in the ass. Not only would he have to determine an alternate blast site, but he was required to report the findings to the historical foundation. They would no doubt send in a group of artifact geeks who would descend on the quarry like a plague of locusts and infect it in a similar way.

The presence of methane had not been detected, but that didn't mean the cave was safe. A small group of engineers and miners were sent into the cavity to determine if the place was structurally sound enough for the scientists to mess around.

Walt Taylor was the first man in; he had served as a tunnel rat in Vietnam and was the best surveyor the company had. The man was as skinny as a birch tree and looked like you could knock him over with a harsh word, but Walt was full of grit and one tough bastard. He inspected the cave and then reported back to Don. "You're not gonna fuckin' like it, boss."

Don braced himself for the bad news.

"There's a ton of stuff in that cave," Walt continued, "artifacts ... all that kinda crap, ya know? It was an important place to someone, tell you what. There's also bones in there, and I mean a fuck load. It could be a burial site. I'm willing to bet those museum guys'll be crawling around in there for months."

Don's stomach did a cartwheel and then turned sour. It was official; the north face had just become a shitshow, and he was the master of ceremonies. He envisioned the ass reaming he would get from old man DuCain and nearly puked. His life was about to become extremely difficult.

"I can do that," Don announced into the phone.

Mark looked up at him through a veil of cigarette smoke.

"Absolutely, I will be sure of that. Okay, I'll be expecting him." He hung up and buried his head in his palms.

"Do I want to know?" Mark put the cigarette out.

"We got a guy coming in on Monday." He checked his scribbled notes. "Dr. Stephen Thompson, curator for the Museum of Natural History, he's supposed to be some type of artifact specialist. We're to give him whatever help he needs."

"What kind of help does he need?" Mark asked. "You go in the cave, you take out the stuff, and you leave."

"Yeah, it isn't as easy as that, apparently. No one is to disturb anything until he gets here."

"What are we supposed to do until then, babysit a hole in the rock?" Mark leaned back in his chair and laced his hands behind his head.

"Well, the guy gets here Monday. It should be easy enough to keep it tight till then. We'll park a dozer in front of the entrance and put up a couple of signs."

The phone rang on Don's desk; both men stared at it for a moment.

"You going to answer that?" Mark asked.

Finally, Don picked up. "Hello, Fischer." A wash of grey drained his face. "Slow down, Lois. What happened?"

Mark furrowed his tangle of brows and looked at his partner.

"Is Troy, okay? Good. He did what? In his pajamas?" Don felt every muscle in his face tighten. "Look, I'm leaving now. I can be there in a half-hour. Is Troy with you? Okay, okay, just try to calm down. I'm on my way." He hung up the phone and bolted from his desk.

"What happened?" Mark asked.

"It's one of Troy's friends; Lois had to bring the kid to Chilton. Found him in the garage in his pajamas."

"What the hell ... pajamas?" Mark winced.

"Look, I'll call you when I know more. Lois is freaking out. I got to go." Don jetted out the door, leaving Mark alone in the trailer.

Lois heard Troy scream from inside the house and knew it was a matter of life or death. She dropped the plate she had been washing and hit the front door at full sprint. She found Troy kneeling over Rob, with the boy convulsing on the garage floor. He was dressed in his pajamas and had started to turn blue. Lois rolled him onto his side and felt the heat radiating from him. His fever had to be close to 105.

"How did he get here?" she asked. "Did he walk all the way in just his pajamas?" Lois looked at Troy, who appeared on the verge of tears and unable to answer.

Nothing made sense, and there was no time; Rob was fading fast. She cradled the boy's head to prevent him from smacking it against the floor as he shook. Then she instructed Troy to retrieve her purse and car keys from inside the house. By the time he returned, Rob had stopped convulsing, and Lois had begun to carry him to the car. Troy helped get him in the back seat, and they sped off. Lois clutched the wheel and prayed; she wasn't sure if Rob would last the two-mile trip to the medical center. *Christ, this kid is on fire.* Now that he was out of the red glow of the garage, Lois could see just how grave he looked. The boy could have already passed for dead; she hoped it wasn't too late. His lips were dark blue, and deep scarlet circles spread out beneath his eyes. The rest of his skin was the dusty white of a corpse. She pushed the Impala's accelerator to the floor, running every traffic light along the way.

She skidded to a halt in the Chilton Medical Center's parking lot in front of the emergency room entrance. Two orderlies rushed to their aid.

Rob was ushered into the emergency room through two batwing doors situated behind an oval reception desk that sat like an island in the center of the large waiting area.

Lois called Rob's parents from the reception desk and tried to explain everything she knew, which wasn't much. Mrs. Boyle had no idea her son had even left the house, and Lois couldn't answer any of her questions. She wasn't sure what had happened herself. The boy had shown up out of nowhere. Minutes later, Karin and Bob Boyle burst through the side entrance and blew past Lois and Troy. They stormed the front desk, where a middle-aged woman sat behind the counter, and were ushered into the emergency room to join their son. Lois and Troy hadn't been allowed in because they weren't family, also because Rob's condition was critical.

They returned to their seats in the waiting area, frantic and in shock, with Troy still wearing his vampire costume and Lois wringing her hands as if they were wet. Minutes later, a young nurse jiggled towards them, her two-sizes-too-small uniform looking more like a coat of white paint.

"Mrs. Fischer, I'm Nurse Gilmartin."

"Yes, how is he?" Lois stood up. "Is he going to be all right?"

"The doctors are with him now. They're trying to bring his fever down. You did good by driving him here. He might not have survived if you waited any longer."

Lois listened and continued to wring her hands.

"His temperature is over 106, but the doctors are doing everything they can. I was hoping you could tell us what happened. Can I get you a cup of coffee or maybe something cold?"

Donald rushed into the building and ran to them. He took Lois in his arms and hugged Troy. "What happened?" he asked, out of breath.

Lois picked up her purse and began to rummage through it. She pulled out a pack of Parliaments. "Mind if I smoke?" After several drags, which appeared to steady her nerves, she did her best to explain what happened, from the moment she heard Troy scream to finding Rob on the cold garage floor. Troy managed to fill in the rest. He told them how Rob had been standing there in a trance and how strange his friend had acted.

"It was like he was coming after me, like he wanted to hurt me. Then when I called to him, it was like he woke up from a dream. He didn't know where he was."

"He's delirious from the fever. I'm surprised he was able to stand at all," the young nurse said.

"I'm sorry." Donald checked the girl's name tag. "Nurse Gilmartin, I'm confused. If Rob is that sick, how the hell did he walk all the way in bare feet and pajamas?"

"I can't answer that, Mr. Fischer." She turned to Troy. "Could I get you a cup of cocoa?"

Troy looked to his father, who nodded his approval.

"I think I'll take you up on that coffee, if that's okay?" Lois added.

Nurse Gilmartin nodded to Donald, who shook his head yes. "I'll be right back," she excused herself and disappeared down the hall.

"What the heck happened, Troy?" Donald asked. "I thought you said he had the flu. How do you think he walked out of the house without his parents even knowing he left?"

"I got no idea, Dad ... really. He didn't come to school, and you should have seen the way he looked at me. I thought he was gonna strangle me or something. He scared the crap out of me."

"Language, Troy," Lois snapped.

"I'm sorry, Mom," he apologized and turned back to his father. "I have no idea how he got there or how long he was even in the garage. He must have been really upset that he missed the party. Maybe he felt good enough to come over."

"In his pajamas? I don't know, kiddo, but I'm proud of you." Donald hugged his son. "That was brave of you tonight. I hope he's going to be okay. His poor parents." He trailed off as Nurse Gilmartin arrived, juggling the coffee and cocoa.

The doctors continued to work on Rob for what felt like half the night. Finally, Karin and Bob exited the emergency room looking haggard and drawn out. They joined the Fischers in the waiting area and filled them in on what they knew so far. Rob's temperature had dropped a few degrees, and he was being given fluids. No one could explain how he had left the house, let alone how he walked nearly a mile in his condition. The doctors were cautiously optimistic at this point and said it was a good sign they were able to bring his temperature down.

The Boyles thanked Lois and Troy for helping Rob and told them there was no reason to stay any longer. They said they would call in the morning with an update. The Fischer family reluctantly left the medical center.

Later, as Troy lay in his bed praying for God to watch over his friend, he replayed the night in his head. It felt like weeks had passed since Wendy kissed him in the garage, though it had only been a few hours. And even though he knew his friend was very sick, something about what happened didn't sit right. It was the way Rob looked at him in the garage and how he had come after him. It felt like Rob had wanted to hurt him. Troy could have sworn Rob had acted as if he was ... hungry. That was it; he had been searching for a way to describe it. Rob had sized him up like a late-night snack.

He lay awake, reliving the scene over and over. It wasn't until much later that Troy was able to fall asleep. He felt like he had just closed his eyes when he woke to the sound of police sirens racing up his street.

CHAPTER 5

Sunday, October 25

At 6:15 a.m., Ted Lutchen found himself at the scene of the first murder in his eighteen-month career as a deputy for the Garrett Grove Sheriff's Department. The clean-cut patrolman, who looked like he had just stepped off the football field after throwing the game-winning touchdown, had responded to several traffic fatalities and even a suicide during his brief time on the force. Garrett Grove was in no way a booming metropolis, and murder had never been a problem before. However, it was 1979 and times were changing. Ted figured if an actor could run for president, then anything was possible, even a murder in Garrett Grove. He proceeded to block off the cul-de-sac at the end of Foothills Drive and put on his most authoritative face. With trembling hands and his heart jackhammering like a greyhound with a case of pre-race jitters, he did his job and prayed the other officers couldn't tell that he was jumpier than a cat in a bathtub.

The victim lay in the street approximately twenty feet from a Con Edison company Ford. Sheriff Carl Primrose and Deputy Gary Forsyth continued to examine the body and the vehicle's contents while they waited for the county coroner to arrive.

Burt Lively had been shaken from his sleep by a phone call from Sheriff Primrose at six twenty. At first, he thought it was a joke ... it had to be. No one got murdered in Garrett Grove. He struggled to shed the sleep from his old, foggy brain and focus on the news coming through the phone line. Then he noticed the alarm in the sheriff's voice and digested the magnitude of the situation. His friend wasn't joking; there had actually been a murder in Garrett Grove. He needed to haul his ass out of bed and get down there right away.

Burt pulled up to the barrier at the end of the block. He jumped out of the black sedan carrying a medical bag. His hair was closer to salt than it was to pepper these days, and it looked as if he hadn't bothered to run a comb through it before leaving the house. The suit jacket he had thrown on was wrinkled and full of lint as if Burt had slept in it. He approached Deputy Lutchen, who moved one side of the wooden police barricade and allowed him to pass through.

"Morning, Mr. Lively." The deputy nodded as the short man passed him in a huff.

Burt joined Sheriff Primrose, who knelt over a large white sheet that covered the body. The sheriff removed his black Stetson cowboy hat, looked up at his old friend, and squinted. Fine lines etched a face that had been weathered more from experience rather than age itself; getting sent to Vietnam had done that to a lot of men his age. "I'd say good morning, Burt, but we both know that's not likely." He pulled the sheet back far enough for the coroner to see. "His name's Felix Castillo, from Warren. He was a lineman for Con Ed."

The dead man lay on his back with his head turned slightly to the right. His eyes were closed, and he almost looked as if he were sleeping. A circular mark on his neck was the only visible wound; several deep punctures dotted the outer edge of the bruise, with one larger incision in the center.

"What do you make of this, Burt?" he asked.

Burt bent down to get a closer look. He took a pair of surgical gloves from his pocket and pulled them on. Then he turned the man's head to examine the other side of his neck and returned it to its original position. The coroner pressed his fingers against the wound and lifted the sheet to examine the rest of the body.

"As far as I can tell, that's the only wound. But I've never seen anything like that before," the sheriff said. "What do you suppose did that?"

Burt lifted the head again, pressed his fingers into the soft flesh of the man's cheek, and released. He examined the pavement near the body and stood up with a confused look. Burt circled the area, then walked to the truck where Deputy Forsyth was busy collecting evidence.

"Howdy, Burt." The deputy removed his yellow-tinted Aviator glasses and offered the coroner a Donny Osmond smile.

The old man ignored him and proceeded to investigate the cab of the truck; Burt mumbled something under his breath and continued to huff. Gary Forsyth watched as the coroner rooted through the cab, searched underneath the seat, and then looked around the passenger's side of the vehicle. Burt paced back to the body and lifted the sheet again. He looked even more confused than he had a moment ago.

"What's going on, Burt? I can see those wheels turning." The sheriff waited patiently.

"I'm confused, Carl," Burt said. They had known each other far longer than either would care to admit and worked together countless times. The old coroner was one of the few individuals in town who called the sheriff by his first name.

"Look at this." Burt put his hands on the man's throat and spread the wound. The large puncture in the center of the circular mark opened, revealing a one-inch slit in the man's neck. "That's his carotid artery." He pointed. "Right there. I can't tell you what the hell made this mark, but I can tell you a couple things right away."

Carl winced. "Well, spit it out. You waiting for me to buy you a goddamn drink, or what?"

The old man took his time examining the victim's head and torso once again. "Well, Carl, you tell me. Where the hell's all the blood? Wound like that, this guy would have bled out like a spigot. There should be one hell of a mess, but I don't see much blood."

A dried smear of dark crimson had crusted at the corner of the man's mouth, and a few drops speckled the area around the wound. Other than that, the only sign of blood was a small spot the size of a silver dollar on the man's shirt, just below the neckline.

"So, what are you telling me, Burt?" Carl squinted his eyes even tighter.

"Well, I see a few possibilities. But none of them make all that much sense. Of course, murders rarely do, but what do I know? I suppose that's your job."

"Oh, for Christ's sake! Would you spill it already!"

"Okay. This guy should have bled like a stuck pig. And unless I'm missing something ... there isn't any blood anywhere. So, the way I see it, either this guy was murdered somewhere else, which is possible—I suppose."

Burt paused to wipe his glasses with a handkerchief he pulled from his jacket pocket and continued. "But ... there's not enough blood on his clothes for that either. So, whoever killed him must've changed his clothes after they whacked him. Oh yeah, they must have washed him up pretty good too 'cause this guy should be covered in blood."

Carl shook his head and grimaced. "I'm not buying any of that. And neither are you."

"Doesn't sound likely," Burt agreed. "By the way the guy's laying, I'd say he didn't put up much of a fight. If I had to guess, he was thrown from over there somewhere." Burt pointed toward the truck. "Just a guess," he continued. "But what I do know? From his skin color and lack of rigor mortis, I can tell you there's very little blood left in his body. Little of anything, for that matter."

Carl looked up and down the street and studied the area of pavement close to the body. "You said there were a few possibilities."

"Well, they all lead to the same result. Someone removed the blood from the body."

Carl shook his head and cringed. "Don't you dare say like a vampire."

"Of course not like a vampire—more like a vacuum cleaner, by the looks of it, big old heavy-duty sucker, at that. Whatever did this was very efficient. You know how messy it can be to drain a body?" He didn't wait for a reply. "Well, I do. Whatever did that was very efficient indeed."

"So, what happened to the blood, Burt?"

"That sounds like police work to me. You'd be looking for about ten or so pints, give or take. I'm guessin' you'll know it when you find it."

"If that's your idea of a joke, I'm not laughing. People don't get murdered in Garrett Grove—not in my town."

"Well, Carl," Burt said, "I hate to tell you, but this guy didn't kill himself, and he didn't die of natural causes. If you ask me, he was murdered. And as far as I know, Foothills Drive is a part of *your* town. So, I guess people do get murdered in Garrett Grove—at least they do now." Burt checked his watch and looked down the street. "The meat wagon will be here soon. I'll let you know what I find out after I perform the autopsy."

Carl took his hat off and ran his fingers through his hair. "You know, Burt, you really got a way of pissing me off." He picked a piece of lint from the black Stetson, then placed it back on his head. "I suppose I don't have to tell you to keep a lid on this."

"I suppose you don't," Burt replied. "But I doubt you'll be able to keep this news from spreading." He nodded toward the barricade, where a group of neighbors were in the process of interrogating Deputy Lutchen.

"Oh Christ." Carl scowled.

"Yeah, you better go take care of that before the kid folds under pressure."

Burt watched as Carl approached the gathering crowd with his hands raised. "Okay, folks, please step back and let us do our jobs." The neighbors retreated to their homes but continued to watch from the safety of their closed windows and drawn curtains. Minutes later, the county coroner's "meat wagon" turned the corner and pulled up to the barricade.

Carl locked eyes with his old friend and shook his head. "What the hell is going on here?" he whispered under his breath as he scanned the neighborhood. "What the hell?"

Ben and Erin Richards had been unable to attend Troy Fischer's Halloween party because they were sick. Their mother, Sally Ann, had stayed up half the night setting cold compresses and monitoring the twins' fevers. The kids had the flu. Erin was running at a steady 102, which had her concerned, but at one point in the night, Ben's temperature had shot to nearly 104. She had put him in a cool bath and given him an adult aspirin, which managed to bring the fever down slightly. But the poor things were miserable. It took Sally Ann everything in her power to get them to eat even a few tablespoons of Lipton Soup. Erin usually loved the Ring-o-Noodles, but tonight, they hadn't eaten a half bowl between them.

The twins continued to toss and turn throughout the night. They sweated through their pajamas and soaked their bedsheets. Sally Ann changed their clothes and watched over them till they both finally fell asleep around 3:30 a.m. Then she retreated to the living room, worrying as only a mother could, and began to nod off herself. Her husband, Dennis, was in their bedroom and managed to sleep through the night undisturbed. Sally Ann had let him; he was currently working nights at the plant, and by the time he dragged himself home every morning, he was exhausted. Saturday into Sunday was his only night off, and she knew if she woke him, he would have been fit to be tied and taken it out on her.

She did everything she could to not aggravate Dennis these days. He never actually hit her, but there were times he had come close and given her a firm shove. Once, he grabbed her arm so hard, the bruises had lasted for two weeks. *It wasn't his fault,* Sally told herself. Dennis was trying so hard to keep the bills paid and food on the table, plus he had a lot of responsibilities at the plant since the layoff. They were lucky he still had a job; nearly half the men at Faber Manufacturing were standing on the unemployment line. Dennis had a right to get a little angry every now and then. Times were tough, and the gas shortage had everyone on edge. Also, Dennis was livid at the idea of an actor running for president.

"I'd vote for Walter Matthau before I voted for Ronald Reagan. Whoever heard of an actor as president? What's next, Sammy Davis Jr. as Secretary of State?!" he screamed one day over the breakfast table.

Sally Ann had listened and agreed with Dennis's rants. What did she know about politics, anyway? She didn't care much about that stuff. She'd liked Kennedy, but that was because she thought he was handsome. These days, she was happy Dennis was still working and she had time to take care of the twins and the house. Besides, Dennis liked things a certain way, and she liked it when he was happy. It was a whole lot better than when he was not.

Last night had been rough, and Sally Ann hoped she could catch a few winks before Dennis woke up. She had an hour or so before he would be looking for his coffee and bacon, just enough time for a little catnap.

Seconds after she closed her eyes, Sally Ann woke to the faint sound of Erin calling for her. The child's voice was whisper-thin. At first, she thought she was dreaming and her daughter was speaking to her from far away. She opened her eyes to find the girl standing nearly on top of her. Erin held out something in her hand to show her mother.

"Mommy." Her voice was barely a breath; she sounded as if she had something in her mouth. "My tooth fell out."

She had to be dreaming; both kids had lost the last of their baby teeth over a year ago. The girl spoke again, finally commanding her mother's full attention.

"Let me see." Sally felt the heat billowing from her. "Oh my God!"

One of Erin's top incisors lay in her hand. The root was red, and there was blood on her palm. Sally opened Erin's mouth to examine her. There was a large gap where her tooth had been.

"Erin, what on Earth happened?" Sally cried.

"I don't know, Mommy; I felt it in my mouth." Erin swayed on her feet, and Sally steadied her.

"Dear God, baby, you're on fire."

"I don't feel good, Mommy." Erin shook for a short second and then bent over and vomited onto the floor.

Sally watched in horror as Erin retched. What came out of the child smelled like death. The little bit of soup she had eaten was expelled in a deluge of dark red blood. She coughed, and a second tooth flew from her mouth and landed in the mess. Sally screamed for Dennis with little concern as to what kind of mood he would wake up in. She scooped up Erin, who immediately began to shake in her arms. "Dennis, wake up!" she screamed again.

Erin began heaving and violently flailing in her arms as Dennis rushed from the bedroom in his boxer shorts.

"What the hell's going on out here? I'm trying to—" He stopped when he saw the state of the living room and his daughter convulsing. He grabbed Erin from Sally and nearly slipped in the vomit. "What happened?"

Before Sally had time to answer, Ben started screaming as if his fingernails were being ripped out with needle-nose pliers.

Dennis stared at his wife with disbelief and panic in his eyes. "Sally," he pleaded. "What the hell is going on?"

Sheriff Primrose was busy instructing his deputies on the steps he wanted taken to secure the crime scene and exactly how he wished the paperwork to be handled when a voice broke over the police band.

"Dispatch to Sheriff Primrose, you out there, Sheriff?" Tara Jefferies called from the station.

"What now?" He reached into the cruiser and grabbed the handset. "Yeah, I'm here. What's up, Tara?"

"Sheriff, there's a problem at the Richards' place on Mountain Ave. Both kids are really sick. Sally Ann called half out of her mind. Pretty serious, by the sound of it, Sheriff. I think the little girl is having a seizure or something ... over."

Carl looked to the end of the cul-de-sac; the Richards' place was only a stone's throw through the woods. "Okay, Tara. I'm right around the corner. I'll meet the ambulance there." Carl jumped into his car.

"10-4, Sheriff, over and out."

"Ted," he shouted to his deputy. "Hop in; you're with me. Gary, secure the scene and get started on the paperwork. Send what you can over to Burt."

"Will do, Sheriff," Deputy Forsyth yelled back.

Sheriff Primrose and Deputy Lutchen sped off down Foothills Drive with the cherries flashing. A minute later, the guys in the meat wagon followed with the body of Felix Castillo bagged and tagged.

Deputy Forsyth approached Burt with the man's credentials in a plastic bag. "I'll log all of this in and get it over to you right away."

"I don't think there's any rush on that, Gary." Burt took off his glasses and wiped them with his hanky. "It's not like he's going anywhere."

"If you say so, Burt." The deputy laughed. "All the same, it won't take long either way."

"You sure about that, Gary? By the looks of it, I'd say you're about to have a pretty busy day." The men could hear the siren from the ambulance as it raced down the Boulevard towards the Richards' house on Mountain Ave.

"Yeah," Gary agreed. "You might be right."

CHAPTER 6

At 4:47 a.m. on Sunday morning, Robert Boyle stopped breathing for nearly three minutes. Dr. Ethan Ziegler, the attending on-call physician, immediately proceeded to administer CPR with the assistance of Head Nurse Doris TenHove. She attempted to breathe life back into the boy as the doctor pumped his chest repeatedly. They had just managed to bring Rob's temperature down a couple degrees when the boy flatlined. His parents were ushered out of the emergency room to allow the staff space to work.

Dr. Ziegler fought to revive Rob until he himself was sweating and out of breath. He was prepared to call the time of death, then pounded on the boy's chest several times with a clenched fist. The child inhaled deeply but struggled to breathe on his own. He was rushed into the ICU, put on a ventilator, and had not regained consciousness.

Rob's face was sallow, and his cheeks had sunken in. Dark circles surrounded his eyes, and his lips were blue. Ziegler ordered a run of full blood work and was waiting for one of the nurses to meet him in the ICU when he was paged over the medical center's intercom system.

"Dr. Ziegler, report to emergency. Dr. Ziegler, report to emergency, code blue."

Ziegler ran toward the double emergency room doors. Blue was the center's code for critical emergency. The soles of his shoes squeaked on the polished tile as he tore through the hallway.

The place was frantic with orderlies, nurses, sheriff's officers, and two patients who had just arrived. Dr. John Malcolm, the chief of medicine, focused his attention on a young girl, while Nurse TenHove attempted to stabilize a boy about the same age. Both children were in the throes of grand mal seizures. The girl dripped blood from her mouth and had more than likely bitten her tongue. Ziegler rushed to the nurse's aid and rolled the boy onto his side to prevent him from hurting himself.

Ziegler recognized the identical symptoms he had witnessed in the Boyle kid. His mind raced to worst-case scenarios and attempted to draw a correlation between the cases. The paramedics ran down a laundry list of symptoms they'd recorded since first entering the home. Ziegler listened but was distracted by the hysterical cries of the children's parents in the waiting room. *What the hell kind of flu is this?* None like he had ever seen. The Boyle kid had been dead for almost three minutes, and these two weren't far off. The boy felt as if he were on fire, and the girl looked as bad as Robert Boyle had. Whatever this bug was, it was nasty as hell.

Ben Richards finally stopped seizing, and Ziegler was able to take his vitals and start an IV. His temperature was 105, and his sister's was over 106. They needed to ice the children and stabilize them as fast as possible. In the adjacent room, he could hear Nurse Gilmartin attempting to calm the frightened parents. But the situation had escalated, and she was losing control by the second. Finally, a booming male voice shouted, "Nobody's gonna stop me from seeing my kids!"

Dr. Malcolm looked up at the sheriff. "Could you help her out there? We can take this from here."

The sheriff and his deputy rushed into the waiting room to diffuse the situation. Badges had a way of grabbing people's attention, especially during times of emergency.

Dr. Malcom lifted the girl's eyelids to find her scleras bloodshot and pupils dilated. He examined her mouth and gasped; the child had lost nearly all her front teeth. Ziegler watched as the chief of medicine examined the girl and checked his own patient. The boy had also lost several teeth, not baby teeth either; the children were losing their permanent bicuspids and incisors.

"Do you see what I'm seeing, Ethan?" Malcolm called to him.

"I see it, Doctor," Ziegler replied. "I have no idea what I'm looking at, but I see it. This isn't any flu. Is it, Dr. Malcolm?"

"None that I've ever seen." Dr. John Malcolm's face drew tighter. "Three children in one night. We need to figure out where the hell these kids have been and who they've been in contact with."

"Wait a second, Doctor. I know where you're about to go with this, and we don't know anything about it yet."

"Exactly!" Malcolm shouted. "We have to act now while there's still a chance to stop it. If it's that contagious, it may already be too late. We need to get everyone who's been in contact with these kids under quarantine. ASAP!"

The staff in the emergency room stared at the chief of medicine as his words echoed like a thunderclap off the stark-sterile walls.

Once the Richards children were stabilized and admitted into the ICU, Dr. Malcolm ordered the wing to be cordoned off. He was headed toward his office when Dr. Ziegler approached him. "Dr. Malcolm, do you think I could have a word with you ... in private?"

Malcolm cast a cautious stare over his bifocals at the young doctor. He liked Ziegler and believed he had a bright future. He still had a way to go, but he was attentive and an excellent diagnostician. What he didn't like about Ethan Ziegler was his cavalier attitude. There was something about the way Ziegler carried himself that rubbed John Malcolm like a sandpaper washcloth. Especially the way he handled himself around the nurses, not to mention, the guy was a bit of a hippie, always looked like he needed a haircut and had to be close to thirty-five.

They walked down the hall together and entered the chief's office. The place smelled like pipe tobacco, and not the cheap kind. Two ornate bookcases stood in the back corners, flanking a wall covered in diplomas, certificates, and awards. A massive dark wooden desk sat at the room's epicenter, serving as John Malcolm's command post.

The old doctor sat behind the desk and held up his hands. "I know what you're about to do; you're going to try to talk me out of calling in the quarantine. But I'm standing my ground on this one."

"No way, Dr. Malcolm. This is your call. You've been in this town a lot longer than I have, and I know you believe this is the best course of action." Ziegler delivered his words with the sincerity of a used car salesman.

Malcolm paused, expecting at least a little resistance. "You're damn right. I'm glad you see it my way."

"Of course. You're the chief of medicine, and I trust your opinion." Ziegler had the same persuasive way with the nurses. "I was just going to suggest a couple scenarios I'm sure you've considered."

Malcolm gave him a puzzled look. "Such as?"

"Well, I was going to mention, since you've decided to initiate quarantine, Sheriff Primrose and his deputy are officially off duty. That's nearly a quarter of this town's police force. Which I imagine could complicate matters?"

John shook his head and leaned back in his chair. "Hmmm." He motioned for Ziegler to continue.

"I imagine it won't be a problem for whoever is at the center already. But you're going to need police officers to find everyone who's been in contact with those kids over the past three days ... possibly longer."

"I know, Doctor. It's one giant mess, but I don't think we have a choice." Malcolm tilted his head and looked down over his bifocals once again. "I take it you have a suggestion, Dr. Ziegler?"

"Well, sir, the Boyle kid has been sick since Thursday. I'm guessing the Richards kids, about the same. None of the parents have taken ill in that time, and the Fischer boy spent the whole week with all three children; he isn't sick either. Surely one of them would have shown symptoms by now."

"We don't know that," Malcolm said.

"I'm just saying this could be something else entirely. We're not going to know until the blood work comes back. And if we cripple the police force, we'll have to call in the state authorities."

Malcolm's furrowed brow softened a bit. "I don't want to see anyone else get sick."

"Chances are it already would have happened." Ziegler blew a piece of hair out of his eyes. "The kids are in the ICU, and no one gets in or out without the proper protection. We'll monitor them around the clock.

That gives us time to run the blood work and rule out everything else before you call it in. In the meantime, tell the sheriff your plans just in case, so he can prepare. We'll instruct everyone to limit their interactions for the next twenty-four hours, just until we know."

Ziegler presented his case with the confidence of a defense attorney. He cleared his throat, adjusted his tie, and continued. "Twenty-four hours of monitoring and tests, full disclosure with the authorities, and if you still feel the same tomorrow, make the call. This way, we'll have a chance to figure things out, and the sheriff will have time to set up whatever preparations he may need as well."

Dr. Malcolm pulled a pipe from his breast pocket and held it for a moment. Then he struck a wooden match and took several puffs of the tobacco. It smelled like cherry and oak. "I hope to God I don't regret this, Ziegler. Twenty-four hours—that's it! If we don't get this thing figured out by then, I'm pulling the plug."

Ziegler smiled. "Great."

"Not so fast." The old doctor took a couple quick pulls from his pipe. "I'm putting you in charge of all the tests. First, I want you to oversee the blood work and go over everything with a fine-tooth comb. Then you'll need to coordinate with radiology, get some chest x-rays, find the kids' dental records, and that's just for starters."

Ziegler appeared to shrink two inches as his chest deflated and shoulders folded inward. "I've been on for almost twelve hours, and I'm scheduled to be off tonight."

"That's not going to be a problem, is it?" Dr. Malcolm didn't wait for an answer. He stood up and headed for the door. "Glad to hear it. I'll check in later to see what you've got," he said and left the office.

Ziegler stood there feeling like he had been kicked in the teeth; somehow, it had blown up in his face. While he honestly believed it was much too soon to initiate a quarantine, his intentions to sway Dr. Malcolm hadn't been selfless. He had plans with Jackie Gilmartin this evening and was pretty sure the young nurse was as eager to see him as he was her. He'd been performing routine examinations on Jackie for a good month now, and tonight, she had promised to leave her nurse's uniform on.

He checked his watch; it was already past eight a.m., and he hadn't eaten anything since well before midnight. He decided to grab a quick cup of coffee and a snack from the cafeteria before seeing Peter in pathology. It was going to be one bitch of a day.

Dr. John Malcolm pulled Sheriff Primrose to the side and spoke to him privately. He told him what he knew so far, what he didn't, and what his plans were if they couldn't come up with anything solid in the next twenty-four hours. Carl thanked him for his discretion and for giving him a fair heads-up before calling in the quarantine. He promised the chief he would make sure the Fischer family were aware of the situation and would talk to them himself to see if anything had been missed. The twins' and Robert Boyle's parents were still at the medical center and agreed to cooperate. It was unlikely any of them would have left the building anyway, not with their children in critical condition and still in the ICU.

The emergency room staff and paramedics who dealt with the twins agreed to limit their contact with the public to a bare minimum for the next twenty-four hours as well. That took care of everyone involved except for Nurse Gilmartin, who had snuck out as soon as her shift ended. Head Nurse TenHove tried to reach the girl repeatedly at her apartment but had been unsuccessful so far. Possibly, she had stopped to get something to eat or pick up a few things at the store before going home. TenHove assured Dr. Malcolm she would continue to try until she contacted the young nurse.

Carl dropped Deputy Lutchen off at the station with strict orders for him to take the rest of the day off and not leave the house. Hopefully, this would all be over soon. If not, they would have a whole lot more to worry about than a lost day of work. Then he contacted Deputy Forsyth to see how the paperwork was coming on the Castillo case. Minutes later, Carl arrived at the home of his former high school sweetheart, Lois Fischer.

CHAPTER 7

Sheriff Carl Primrose pulled into the driveway and sat for a moment listening to the steady hum of the police cruiser. He had spent a long time trying to forget the past and was completely unprepared when it snuck up and sucker punched him. It all came back in a vivid wash as if it were yesterday.

Lois met Donald Fischer during her sophomore year at Penn State while she and Carl had been attempting to prove that a long-distance relationship could actually work. The truth was they seldom did, and by the time Lois returned to Garrett Grove, she and Carl were history. Not that he had wanted it that way; for Carl, Lois was the love of his life, and he never fully got over it.

"It will be good for us to spend some time apart," she had told Carl the week before she left for college. "By the time we see each other again, you won't be able to resist me."

Carl had parked the Mustang at the top of Mountain Ave. It was a favorite spot for teens even in '67. "I can't resist you now," he had said. "I don't see how being apart could possibly help."

Lois had her heart set on going to Penn State and been on cloud nine when she got accepted; it was all she could talk about. "We'll see each other on holidays and over the summer. Oh yeah, don't forget spring break. You'll see; things won't be all that different." And she had believed every word of it.

From the top of Mountain Ave, they could see the floodlights over the high school football field and damn near all of Garrett Grove. The moonlight glinted off the steeple of the Lutheran church and lit up the Lenape River as if it were the Ganges. But it all struck Carl as out of focus and not nearly as bright as it had in the past.

"Maybe I should apply to Penn State? Who knows, I might get accepted." But Carl knew that was a pipe dream; he didn't have the grades for it.

"You'd hate it, and you know it." She leaned over and kissed him while the Beatles played through the Mustang's A.M. radio, a sappy ballad about how far away all of Paul McCartney's troubles seemed. It was surreal. "I could never forgive myself for making you miserable."

"I wouldn't be miserable. I'd be with you," he assured her but knew he was lying.

"What about the sheriff's department? It's all you've talked about for the last two years. You're just gonna throw that away?"

Carl had known she was right; he'd wanted to be a deputy for a lot longer than two years. His father had been the sheriff of Garrett Grove, and Carl planned to follow in his footsteps. It had been his dream since he was old enough to see out the windshield of his father's police cruiser from the safety of the old man's lap. Allan Primrose had let his son hit the siren and flash the lights every time they drove past Bell's Hardware. It made Carl feel special, and he wanted to be just like his dad. Sheriff Primrose, the first, was a well-respected man in town and for good reason. He went out of his way to help people simply because he liked to do it. And Carl was a chip off the old block. He couldn't imagine a better job than helping and protecting the people in his own town.

"You're going to be Sheriff of Garrett Grove one day, and you're going to be damn good at it," Lois told him. "I can't let you give that up for me. I just couldn't live with that."

"I can't live without you, Lois. I love you."

"I love you too."

That night, they made love in the Mustang at the top of Mountain Ave. It hadn't been their first time, and probably not even the last. But looking back, Carl thought it was the last time that counted.

Lois went to Penn State, and they called each other every day, at first. She came home for the holidays, and he'd even driven there a few times to see her. Then she decided to take a few summer courses. After that, they began to talk less and less. A minute here, five minutes there. The calls became more infrequent. Carl tried to reach out every chance he could but found her either heading off to class or busy with homework.

When she called him out of the blue one day, he could tell right away by the sound of her voice and knew what she was about to say. Lois said she was sorry, that she still loved him and didn't want to hurt him.

"Well, don't do it then!" he yelled over the phone. "I knew this was going to happen, and what did you say? You said it would be good for us. You said it would make us closer." He could hear her crying on the other end.

"I'm so sorry. I still love you, Carl."

"So, what's the problem then, Lois?" She didn't answer him.

She had started to cry, then finally blurted it out: "I'm pregnant, Carl."

He had to think about it for a moment, and then it hit him. Carl hadn't seen her in over four months. Lois had been seeing someone else, and the prick had knocked her up.

"What's his name?" The phone had grown heavy in his hand as arctic waves leached through the earpiece into his head. *How can you do this to me? You—you're my life. I—I can't.*

"D ... Donald," she said between sobs.

"Do you love him?" he asked again, and again, he waited for a reply.

"You're not saying. So, either you don't, or you don't want to tell me that you do." He had wanted to scream but knew it would only make things worse.

"I guess that's it then?" He waited for her to say something otherwise, but she never did. He had lost her, the only girl he had ever loved and ever would.

"I'm sorry, Carl. You deserved better." Her words, nearly impossible to make out through her tears. "I love you," she said and hung up the phone.

He had stood there frozen with his heart bleeding inside his chest. All the years, every dream they had shared, was over. Carl had been certain his world would never be the same ... and he had been correct. Three weeks later, he was drafted and sent to fight in Vietnam.

It was strange that he could remember it all so vividly. The sting was still bitter, although it had mellowed with age. *Time heals all ... almost.* Carl did his best to shake it off and focus on the matter at hand. This was no time to be floating around in the clouds. There had been a murder with an unexplainable cause of death. Now, three kids were clinging to life in the ICU with something possibly a whole lot worse than the flu.

He turned off the cruiser's ignition and pushed all thoughts of his high school sweetheart to the back of his mind. That was until he saw Lois standing in her kitchen, and the memories flooded back like the Lenape River during storm season.

Butchie Post watched Jackie Gilmartin from the front seat of his Chevy Monza as she entered Wilson's Diner at nine a.m. Sunday morning. Her nurse's uniform clung to her hips, but Butchie focused on the way it showed off her giant tits. He thought they looked like cantaloupes wrapped in white cotton. Jackie hadn't looked half as good back in high school; she hadn't blossomed yet. She sure as hell hadn't had tits like that, or Butchie would have noticed.

In truth, Jackie had started to bloom her senior year, but Butchie had been kicked out by then. He got expelled during the middle of his sophomore year, which was fine by him. School was for pussies anyway. And it had been that douchebag Jimmy Reilly's fault; he was the one who had gotten Butchie kicked out in the first place.

Butchie entered the world as Marion Arthur Post but adopted the moniker Butchie for obvious reasons. His mother named him Marion; she said that his father resembled the Duke. Butchie never met his dad, at least not that he could remember. The guy skipped out when Butchie was still shitting his diapers. He'd seen a couple pictures of Mark Post but didn't think the guy looked anything like John Wayne. What the hell was his mom thinking when she married him, anyway? Butchie figured she must have been drunk that year. Why would that year be any different than the rest?

He chose the name Butchie after watching *Butch Cassidy and the Sundance Kid*. Now that was one cool-ass cowboy, not no pussy like John Wayne. He had taken a lot of shit as a kid with the name Marion, not to mention he was the only boy in the class without a dad.

"Mary, Mary, look at the fairy." One of the many brilliant limericks the children had created to tease him. Another incredibly original one was "Marion the Fairion, where's your daddy, little girl?". It didn't rhyme, but it had the same effect.

The taunts and constant name-calling had hurt. And when he told the other children his name wasn't Marion, it was Butchie, it only made the teasing worse. That had gone on well into the third grade, but by then, Butchie experienced an early growth spurt. Also, getting left back in the second grade gave him the advantage of brute strength over his younger classmates. Then one day, he discovered he had the power to shut their twisted pussy pie holes. And he liked the way it felt.

Joey Turner and Gilbert Duncan had been ripping Butchie for a good week. The two boys followed him home from school one day, taunting him as he walked up the Boulevard towards Foothills Drive.

"Mary, Mary, quite contrary. Why you such a fucking fairy?"

Butchie pretended not to hear them as he walked toward his house on Mountain Ave. But the boys keep calling to him, over and over.

"Hey, Mary. I heard your momma's a drunk; that's why your daddy left her."

Butchie had started crying. They had no right to talk about his mother, and he could feel the pressure building up inside him like a teapot just before it started to whistle. He walked faster, but the children continued to follow.

"Mary, Mary." The boys matched his pace.

"Hey, where are you going, Mary?"

Butchie took off running, and Joey and Gilbert chased after him. He pumped his legs as fast as he could but knew they were closing in. He approached the shortcut through the foothills and decided to take it. He turned left onto the dirt path and into the woods. Joey followed him with Gilbert right behind.

"Hey, sissy, where are you going?" Joey called.

"Yeah, don't run, mommy's boy," Gilbert yelled.

Butchie's lungs burned, and his heart threatened to explode. His fear escalated to the tipping point. Then, a thunderous crack erupted inside his head, loud and concussive. He howled, sounding more like a wild animal caught in a trap than a frightened little boy. Joey and Gilbert realized a second too late they were in deep shit, as Butchie turned and went ballistic.

First, Butchie slammed his clenched fist into Joey's jaw as the child tried to stop short. The force of the blow and the pursuing child's own momentum resulted in one bad-ass wallop. Joey's feet flew out from under him, and he landed hard on his back. Gilbert didn't have time to stop either and nearly ran over his friend. Which gave Butchie enough time to seize him by the hair on the back of his head. He dragged Gilbert off the path and ran him face-first into the nearest tree. Gilbert fell to his knees, screaming, with his nose shifted almost two inches to the left and spouting like a geyser.

Butchie turned back towards Joey, who was struggling to get to his feet.

"Okay, okay. I'm sorry; stop it! I'm sorry!" the boy cried.

Butchie bent down and picked up a branch about two inches thick and three feet long. He checked how it felt in his hand and took a couple practice swings as he walked back to where Joey scrambled.

He raised the log above his head and brought it down on Joey's shoulder. The boy's collarbone snapped like a toothpick. Butchie smiled when the child screamed. He raised it again and brought it down harder the second time.

"My name is BUTCHIE!" he yelled as he slammed the stick down on the child's ribs.

"My name is BUTCHIE!" Into his stomach.

"BUTCHIE!" His knees.

After that day, there wasn't a soul in Garrett Grove who would so much as look at him sideways, let alone call him anything other than Butchie. Marion Arthur Post was dead. Long live Butchie the Destroyer.

Joey and Gilbert eventually healed, but their experience was a lesson for all. Butchie had stuck up for himself that afternoon, and everything changed after that. Soon, he began to look for fights, just to add a little excitement to his day. He had taken crap for so long, and now that the shoe was on the other foot, he liked just how comfortable it felt. He was good at beating the snot out of pussies, enjoyed it too. And why shouldn't he? They had it coming. It wasn't long before Butchie started getting suspended for fighting.

How Butchie had gotten as far as high school without getting kicked out sooner was an accomplishment in itself. And to have made it into his sophomore year was nothing short of a miracle. The teachers and principal felt somewhat sorry for the boy. His father had abandoned him, and his mother had a bit of a problem with the bottle. Who wouldn't be a little angry? However, Butchie Post wasn't just a little angry; Butchie was disturbed, and not just a little. The boy was a raging psychopath. He was constantly in trouble for one thing or another. On one occasion, he smashed the windows of his English teacher's car and spray-painted the words *Die Pussy* on the hood. There was the constant fighting, of course, but the final straw was the day he waited in the boy's bathroom for Jimmy Reilly.

He targeted Jimmy earlier that year and made the kid's life a living nightmare. Just before Jimmy entered the bathroom, Butchie lit a cherry bomb and threw it into the toilet. Unfortunately for Jimmy, the firecracker went off just as he opened the stall. Butchie couldn't have timed it better.

The ceramic shattered as the cherry bomb exploded, sending lacerating pieces of the broken toilet flying in every direction. Jimmy's face looked like he'd been run through a blender. And that was the end of Butchie Post's academic career; he was expelled, and Jimmy's parents pressed charges. Butchie spent eighteen months in the Barre Oaks Youth Correctional Facility. And almost lasted a whole day without getting into trouble. But Butchie learned fast that no matter how tough you thought you were, there was always someone tougher.

Butchie had been beating on smaller kids from the backwoods-sticks of Garrett Grove. He hadn't faced any real resistance yet and thought he was hot shit. But Barre Oaks housed boys as old as eighteen from all over the state. Cities like Millville and Burlington were home to some pretty rough neighborhoods. Nothing like the small town Butchie had grown up in.

The biggest problem that followed Butchie into the correctional system was his government name, Marion. The guards as well as the inmates seized the opportunity and ran with it. He arrived on a bus full of young men ranging in age from fifteen to eighteen. Butchie was at the younger end of the spectrum but by no means the smaller. And he probably would have been fine if it hadn't been for the name and the giant chip on his shoulder.

The new recruits were stripped, thrown into a cold shower, and processed. Butchie was approached by a guard that towered over him by a good two feet, with a forehead the size of a cinderblock that protruded nearly as far as his chin. The Neanderthal looked down at his clipboard and burst out laughing.

"Marion Post," he yelled loud enough for the other cops, as well as the busload of new inmates, to hear. "Marion?"

"It's Butchie," he said.

"Did you say something? I didn't tell you to speak, Marion," the cop barked in Butchie's face. Three of the goon's cronies closed in around Butchie like sharks circling a wounded seal.

"You want to repeat that, Marion?" the cop screamed. Spit flew from his mouth onto Butchie's face.

Butchie may have been hard-headed, but he wasn't a complete idiot. He knew there was nothing to be gained from an encounter with Mighty Joe Young and his band of merry dicks. He shook his head and looked at the floor.

"That's what I thought, Marion." The cop flipped through his paperwork. "Dorm three, bunk seven. Next!"

That's how it started, and it only got worse from there. The boys had to walk naked and barefoot to their dorms through the entire complex. The inmate population screamed and whistled as they passed. Some threw toilet paper and food at the new fish, and by the time Butchie arrived at dorm three, he was covered in ketchup and pop and in need of another shower.

He quickly learned of a strange phenomenon in the prison system: gossip traveled faster here than it did at the beauty salon. By the time he reached the dorm, there wasn't a soul in the facility who didn't know his name was Marion.

The first fight happened in the shower. Two guys, who didn't look like much of a threat, began ribbing him about the name. Butchie stuck up for himself and taught them a pretty good lesson, leaving one with a shiner and the other with a busted lip.

"My name's, Butchie," he spat and figured it was over.

But it was far from over. The two guys he fought were low-ranking members of the Bristol Boys, and the rest of the gang didn't appreciate that some guy named Marion had bested two of their own. Later that night, they followed Butchie from the mess hall and jumped him when he passed the woodshop, dragging him inside. Butchie squared off and stood his ground. "I'm not afraid. I'll fight all of you," he had said.

One of them seized him from behind as two others grabbed each of his arms.

"Let me go," he screamed. "I'll take all of you."

A large Italian-looking kid with greasy black hair and an even greasier face stepped up. Butchie figured the kid had to be the leader as he struggled to free himself.

"You're right about that," the kid said. "You will *take* all of us."

Butchie didn't follow what the guido meant until the other three pushed him to the floor face first. He tried to free himself, but there were too many of them. One of the boys grabbed the back of his jumper and yanked at it. The material ripped easily, exposing him. Then they were tearing at his boxer shorts. *What the hell are they trying to do?* Then it hit him. They were trying to do him. The guido knelt over Butchie while the others held him down, then he took him.

He had never been with a woman in his life and had never known his father. His first sexual experience was on the cold concrete floor of the woodshop in Barre Oaks. After the first boy finished, the next one jumped on him, and then the next.

They laughed and called him Marion as they raped him, then left when they were done. He lay there for nearly an hour, seething with rage and humiliation. A bitter morass like no other clawed its way inside him. It gripped Butchie's black heart and twisted. And had there been an ounce of humanity left in Butchie Post prior to that moment, it had been silenced once and for all that night on the woodshop floor.

The Bristol Boys were by no means the only predators who stalked the halls of Barre Oaks. And although they were deviant in their idea of hierarchy, they followed a specific code, and they took care of their own. Butchie's service to the gang had turned out to be some insane form of initiation. He continued to fight back and got his knuckles bloody when the opportunity presented itself. But he also took his beatings and nights on the woodshop floor and kept his mouth shut. He never said a word, primarily out of humiliation but also out of pride. It was evident the Bristol Boys had found a new recruit, and everyone in the facility knew what that involved. All the while, Butchie stayed to himself and took it like a man ... so to speak.

Vinnie, the leader of the group who had introduced himself most intimately that first night, had taken a liking to Butchie. And not in the obvious sense. Vincenzo "Vinnie" Rozgoni from Millville respected how Butchie stood up to him and always tried to get a few licks in first. Most of all, he respected how the guy kept his mouth shut. Other fish usually sang after the first time. Of course, they were dealt with accordingly. But Butchie was different, and Vinnie liked that. The kid had passed his initiation.

Butchie had been picking up cigarette butts outside the administration building when Vinnie and another boy, who was built like a brick shithouse and looked about as bright as one, approached him. Butchie prepared to defend himself; he dropped the bag of butts and clenched his fists.

"Relax, Post. I want to talk." Vinnie stopped in front of him.

Butchie expected the other guy to grab him or hit him from behind. He watched the kid, ready to knock out a few of his teeth.

"I got something going on tonight. Some prick over on A Unit needs to learn who runs this place. Want a chance to be on top?" Vinnie asked.

After all that Butchie had been through in the past three months, it was hard to believe that Vinnie was being straight with him. *Is he asking me to join the Boys?* It sure sounded like it, but did it mean what he thought? Judging from what the group had done to him, Butchie figured as much.

"This is a one-time offer. I ain't gonna ask twice." The boys stood there waiting for Butchie to reply.

There was a good chance they were just messing with him and decided to add a whole new element of foreplay to the game. But there was also a chance that Vinnie was on the up and up. Either way, Butchie figured he had nothing to lose. Not like his situation could get much worse.

"I'm in," he said.

An evil grin spread across Vinnie's greasy face like a germ. He held his hand out to Butchie, who reluctantly shook it.

After chow, he met up with the gang in the bathroom on A Unit. Butchie half expected them to jump him and laugh at what a sucker he had been, but that's not what happened. An older red-headed boy entered the bathroom with his chest puffed out and arms held a distance from his body, as if his biceps were too big to walk right. A real cocky douchebag, by the looks of it, and Butchie disliked the guy the second he saw him.

"Get 'em, boys!" Vinnie shouted, then waited as the rest of the gang swarmed their new target like a colony of fire ants.

"Not so tough now, are you, Cunningham?" Vinnie approached the cocky ginger before the kid could say a word and shoved a rolled-up sock in his mouth. A dirty one, by the looks of it. The Bristol Boys wrestled him to the floor, tore at his jumper, and stripped him. Finally, Vinnie turned to Butchie, who, up until that point, had only been watching. "Let's see what you got, Post," he said.

Butchie didn't need to be told twice and had gotten worked up seeing someone else face down on the floor for a change. Turned out, it wasn't any different than what he had learned that day in the woods. The day he finally stood up to Joey and Gilbert. It felt a whole lot better to give it than it did to take. And Butchie gave it like a champ; he passed his initiation with flying colors and enjoyed himself in the process ... very much, in fact.

That had been almost ten years ago. Now, as Butchie watched Jackie Gilmartin enter Wilson's Diner, he visualized the look in her eyes when he finally got the chance to shove a rolled-up sock into her mouth. He pictured himself forcing her to the floor of his shed and ripping the back of her nurse's uniform at the seams. A quick glance at his watch told him the supermarket had been open for fifteen minutes. Butchie had lost track of time, awash in the sourness of his thoughts. The girl would have to wait. The shed behind his house wasn't going anywhere, neither was the roll of duct tape in his glove compartment. He'd been following Jackie for the past two weeks, waiting for just the right moment. But this wasn't it. He needed to pick up a few things for his mother and something special for himself. He hoped Jackie was patient and swore he would make it up to her. She was going to love what he had done with the shed. He just knew it.

Butchie exited the car and walked into the A&P supermarket. He caught a glimpse of his reflection in the sliding door and liked how he looked, his big barrel chest and squared-off jaw. If he hadn't grown his hair into a mullet, he could have passed for that cowboy in the movies, the one with the eye patch in *True Grit*. Butchie couldn't remember the actor's name and imagined he was probably just another Hollywood pussy.

He grabbed what he needed and left the store, immediately noticing Jackie's car was no longer in front of Wilson's. He stepped onto the sidewalk and stopped short. Two kids had parked their bicycles right next to his Monza. Butchie's blood sizzled when he saw the little homos walking into the candy store. They had left their bikes propped up on the kickstands, right there on the sidewalk—as if they owned the damn place.

Butchie stormed over to where the first bike was set up, his bags of goodies clutched tightly in his arms. He raised his foot and kicked the bike over with a firm boot to the seat. The two boys looked back in horror as the bicycle crashed to the sidewalk. Tommy Negal saw the man had kicked over Jeff Campbell's bike and couldn't help but laugh. But he was immediately sorry he did.

Butchie turned to him and screamed, "Don't you fucking laugh. I'll knock yours down too." He kicked Tommy's bike with every ounce of tainted fury in his black heart. It crashed to the pavement like a lead balloon. Then Butchie spit on the bikes, got into his car, and peeled away from the curb.

CHAPTER 8

Troy sat at the breakfast table, pushing scrambled eggs from one side of his plate to the other. He wasn't hungry but pretended to enjoy it for the benefit of his parents. The past twelve hours had been difficult to process, and Troy wasn't sure he had even fallen asleep. But he figured he must have because he remembered dreaming about sirens.

The party had been a hit, and all his friends loved Scream in the Dark. Mike and Tommy cried like little girls when Billy and Eric chased them down the street. Troy snickered just thinking about it, then recovered and shoved a forkful of eggs into his mouth. And Wendy had kissed him! *Did that really happen?* The entire night felt like a dream. *It sure did!* She asked to see the haunted house, just the two of them, and then ... *Wham!* It was weird at first; she'd caught him by surprise, and he didn't know what he was supposed to do. Then it happened again. Troy thought he might have done a better job the second time. He knew the older kids did something with their tongues called French kissing. But didn't think he would like that very much; it sounded gross. He grimaced at the runny eggs on his plate.

For weeks, he'd imagined what the night of the party would be like. Ever since Rob had come up with the name for the haunted house, Scream in the Dark. He thought it would turn out awesome, and it had, but not in a million years did he think that Wendy would actually kiss him. He couldn't wait to tell Rob.

Troy's stomach soured at the thought of his friend, and he lost what little was left of his appetite. It must have killed Rob to miss the party. He was probably so upset, he got out of bed and walked over in his pajamas just to join them. Too bad everyone had already left. But Rob had been really sick and looked terrible, even scarier than Troy did with his vampire makeup on.

And there was something else about the way Rob looked at him. *It was like he didn't even see me.* Then Rob had lifted his arms and come after him. It was as if—

"Troy, eat your breakfast," Lois said.

"I'm not very hungry," he replied.

"Eat up, sport," Don added. "There are children in Africa who are starving."

"They can have the rest of my eggs," he pouted.

Don and Lois exchanged a stifled laugh. That had been a good one; they both nodded. Lois pushed Troy's hair out of his eyes. It was getting long, and he needed it cut. "Just one more bite. Do it for me?" she asked.

Troy scooped a forkful into his mouth and bounded from the table as if he had been released from the electric chair. He took his plate to the garbage and scraped the rest of his breakfast into the can. A loud knock at the front door caused all of them to jump.

"I'll get it," Troy shouted, running out of the kitchen.

Sheriff Primrose stood on the front porch with his cowboy hat in his hands. "Good morning, Troy." He smiled. "How are you feeling today, partner?"

"Hi, Sheriff Primrose. I'm good, thanks; we were just finishing breakfast."

"I hope I didn't come at a bad time."

"Not at all, Sheriff," Don called from the kitchen. "You're just in time for coffee. Come on in."

Troy opened the screen door and let him in as Lois looked around the corner. "Milk and sugar, Carl?" she offered. They had worked past much of the awkwardness years ago, for the most part.

"Just black," Carl said, ascending the steps leading to the bi-level's second floor, two at a time.

"How are things at Chilton?" Lois asked. "I haven't heard from Karin or Bob and didn't want to call just yet. You know, if—"

"That's why I'm here, actually." He rolled his eyes in Troy's direction, and Lois understood what he was implying.

"Troy, do you think you could see if the paper is here yet?"

Troy headed out the front door as Don poured the coffee. "So, what's going on, Sheriff? We heard the sirens earlier, and I'm guessing you didn't stop by for Lois's coffee."

Carl took a seat at the table and set his hat on an empty chair.

"No, that's not why I'm here." He paused, taking a sip from his mug. "What I'm about to say doesn't leave this room. Not a word."

Lois raised a hand to her lips. "Oh my God, Robert didn't—"

"The boy is in ICU at the moment." Carl stopped her. "The doctors are running tests on the other kids as well."

"Kids?" Don raised his voice. "What do you mean, other kids?"

"The Richards twins were rushed into the emergency room early this morning. They're showing similar symptoms. Doctor Malcolm believes we might have a situation here. How are you both feeling? How about Troy?"

Lois and Don looked at each other as if the oven had exploded. "We're fine," Don said. "Everyone's fine. We're still talking about the flu, aren't we, Sheriff?"

"The truth is they don't know yet. And if we can't get it figured out quick, we might be looking at a quarantine. That means the three of you and everyone else who was there last night."

"Dear God!" Lois gasped and covered her heart.

"I need you folks to stick around the house today, at least until Malcolm gets a handle on this." He decided not to say how the Boyle kid had nearly died last night and wasn't about to tell them how the Richards twins were losing teeth faster than a couple of hockey players. "I'm sure he'll have this straightened out by the end of the day. Just here to cover all the bases. If you guys could avoid going out or seeing anyone, I'd really appreciate it."

"We were going to go to church at ten, but I'm sure Troy won't mind if we miss one Sunday." Carl could see Don was trying to sound calm but was on the verge of freaking out. Lois, however, was having a harder time of it.

"They must have some idea what it is. Rob had the flu. He was delirious and had a fever, but it was just the flu, right?" she said, her voice rising slightly.

Carl looked across the table at her. She was scared, and she had every right to be. "More than likely." He tried to reassure her. "You know how Dr. Malcolm can be. This is just a precautionary measure, probably all for nothing."

"You're probably right." Lois relaxed a little. "Doc can be a little much at times."

Carl turned to Don. "Would you mind if I asked Troy a couple questions about last night? I'd like to see if he saw something we might have missed, if it's okay with you."

"I guess." Don hesitated. "Sure, no problem."

"Paper's not here yet," Troy shouted as he entered the house.

"Hey, Troy," Don called. "Why don't you show the sheriff all the work you did on the haunted house?"

Troy ran into the kitchen; his mood suddenly lifted an inch or two. "It's called Scream in the Dark. Rob came up with the name. We did all the work ourselves, and I thought up the rat room."

"Rat room?" Carl stood up from the table. "I have to see this."

Troy's eyes lit up as he led the sheriff out the front door.

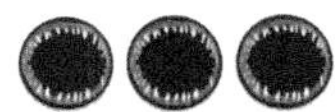

Billy and Eric Tobin were told by their father that neither of them would be leaving the house until the backyard was raked and the leaves were bagged. Billy had been up all night trying to understand what happened at the sanatorium but had no luck so far. He woke to find a note from his father, reminding him about the yardwork, and decided to get an early jump on the leaves. Eric was still dragging his ass inside.

They'd been there countless times before, and nothing like that had ever happened. Sure, the place was spooky, but that was the whole idea. It was easier to comfort a girl out of her panties after she had a good scare and a couple beers. And since Halloween was only a week away, it seemed like the perfect place to bring their dates.

But something was up there, and it had chased them down the mountain. Billy didn't have a clue what it might have been, but it was fast as fuck. And it flew over their heads like a goddamn screaming eagle or something. It was big, whatever it was.

He spent more than half the night trying to piece it all together and still had no idea what it could have been.

When the thing initially passed through the beam of the flashlight, it didn't look real. Billy tried to remember what he had seen as he raked the same pile of leaves for a second time. It hadn't been solid; it was more like ... He tried to remember. Then it hit him. *Smoke!* It had looked like smoke when it passed through the light, not solid enough to make a shadow and not entirely there.

"Do you hear yourself?" he said out loud. "Smoke?"

He tried to shake off the idea, but it held firm. Whatever was up there had waited for them, just beyond the reach of the light, as if it were intelligent.

"It freaking chased us," he whispered. *What's smart and fast and can fly like that?* It had to be an owl or some big-ass bird of prey. That was probably it, one big-ass bird of prey.

Eric finally stepped outside with sleep in his eyes and his hair a mess. "You're up early," he said.

"Butt-munch, it's almost ten o' clock. We should be halfway done by now," Billy told his younger brother.

"I couldn't sleep. That shit scared the living crap out of me last night." Eric grabbed a roll of hefty bags and tore one open.

"You and me both. I still can't figure out what the hell was out there. Some kind of bird, I guess." Billy dropped the rake and walked over to Eric. "It freaking flew over us, right? Then it waited for us like it was smart."

"I don't give a crap what it was. I should have never let you talk me into going up there in the first place." Eric rubbed a sleep crumb from his eyes.

Billy punched him hard enough in the bicep to cause Eric to drop the bags.

"Asshole, whatcha do that for?"

Billy shouted at him. "You wanted to go up there just as much as I did, dickweed. Don't say you didn't!"

"You didn't have to hit me, for Christ's sake," Eric whined.

"Stop being such a baby. I'm trying to make some sense out of this shit, and you're not helping."

"Okay, I don't know, yeah, maybe it was a bird, a smart bird. Is that better?"

Billy wanted to hit him again but managed to hold back. There was barely a two-year age difference between them, but sometimes it felt like a thousand. Eric had always been the baby of the family, and it still showed. He never took anything seriously, and Billy didn't think he stood much of a chance with Susan Smith. It wouldn't be long before she got tired of Eric's idiotic behavior.

On the other hand, Billy figured he might be giving Susan a little too much credit. She had been unfazed by Eric's antics. In fact, she appeared enamored with his crap. Maybe the girl was just as much of a dipshit as Eric.

"I just want to figure out what the hell it was," Billy explained.

"I get what you're saying, Bill. I'm just saying that I don't really give a fuck. It chased us, and it scared the shit out of me. I'm never going up there again, and that's what I think." Eric had a point, but it still pissed Billy off.

"Mick could have been killed last night. Don't you feel like we should go back and look around, try to figure out what the hell is up there?" Billy tried to guilt his brother a little.

"NO! No, I don't feel that way at all. I feel like we should forget about that fucking place, go back to school tomorrow, and never talk about it again. That's how I feel about it."

"I'm going up there, and you're coming with me." Billy pulled the older brother card, the trump card. "We're gonna finish raking these leaves, grab Mick, and we're going back to the sanatorium, and that's final."

Eric didn't continue to fight. There was no use; Billy had played his hand, and there was no way to win after that. "As long as we're back before it gets dark, and we bring one of the shotguns." Those were his demands.

"Oh yeah," Billy agreed. "We're gonna bring a couple of 'em."

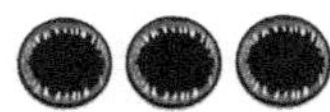

Carl followed Troy into the garage. He didn't know what to expect and was taken aback by the amount of detail he saw. It was hard to imagine that a couple of ten-year-olds had built it themselves. The place had definitely taken a great deal of hard work. They entered into a tight hallway with a cage window set into one of the walls.

"I stopped here." Troy showed the sheriff. "It was really dark, and no one could get past me. Then Billy turned on the strobe light and the tape recorder. Billy and Eric were in the cage, and they tried to grab everyone."

"I bet that scared the pants off your friends." Carl had to admit the kid had done a hell of a job. "Did you think of that yourself?"

"Yeah, that was my idea," Troy boasted. "Me and Rob built the whole place in just a couple days."

"I'm impressed. You've got quite a talent. Might want to get into the movie business someday."

"What do you mean?" Troy raised his eyebrows.

"Well, they have guys in the movie business called set designers who build everything you see on film. They make the haunted houses, the laboratories, sometimes they even build entire towns. Sounds like something you'd be darn good at."

"You really think so?" An epic smile filled his entire face. "You think I could do that?"

"I think you could do anything if you put your mind to it," Carl said, patting Troy on the back.

"Gee, thanks, Sheriff." Troy showed him into the spider room and explained how the plastic arachnids were suspended from the ceiling by lengths of fishing line that ran into a secret hallway on the other side of the room. Eric operated a wheel from inside the hidden space and had lowered the spiders onto the children's heads. The hallway was a small tunnel where all the secrets to Scream in the Dark were hidden. It was where the rats and spiders were operated, and it allowed access to the cage. It also served as a command center where the Tobin brothers could work the strobe light and boom box.

The next room was even more involved than the first two and showed off the level of creativity the boys possessed.

"Where did you get these ideas, Troy?" Carl asked as he tried to navigate the rubber hoses. It was easy to imagine he was walking over rats. With the added effects of darkness and tape-recorded rodents, the kids must have been terrified.

"Once, I was walking in the backyard and stepped on the garden hose. I got scared because it felt like I squished a mouse or a snake. I thought it would be even scarier in the dark; pretty cool, huh?"

"Pretty cool indeed."

They stepped into the graveyard room, and Carl took it all in. "Is this where you found Rob?"

"Yeah, I was taking out the garbage, and I heard something. I thought maybe it was a raccoon. So, I walked in, and he was standing right there." Troy pointed toward the corner of the room beyond the headstones. "He was just kinda staring at the wall."

"What happened then?" Carl asked.

"Well, I wasn't sure it was him. I think I said hello."

Carl listened as he stepped over the small fence into the graveyard. He scanned the room, from the red bulbs on the wall to the materials used to construct the fence and coffin. He noticed the cardboard headstones that read I.P. Daily and Bob Frapples. *Genius.* He laughed and looked back at Troy. "Then what happened?"

"He turned around, and I saw it was him. He looked terrible. Rob was supposed to dress as the vampire. He was gonna jump out of the coffin."

"In there?" Carl pointed at the coffin.

"Yeah, that's when I saw how bad he looked. He had big circles under his eyes, and his face was like a ghost."

"I bet it was pretty scary to see him like that," Carl said, bending down to take a closer look inside the coffin.

"Not until he tried to grab me," Troy stated.

"What do you mean, tried to grab you?" Carl raised his head.

"He didn't recognize me at first; it was like he was in a trance. Then, he started walking towards me and put his arms up like this." Troy held his hands out like Frankenstein's monster. "Then he hissed and tried to grab me."

Carl furrowed his brow in disbelief.

"Then ... it was like he woke up and didn't know where he was."

"You think he was sleepwalking?"

Troy thought about it for a second. "I guess so. I mean ... yeah. He was probably sleepwalking. Um, Sheriff, do you think Rob is gonna be okay?"

Carl nodded and offered a thin smile. "I'm sure your friend is going to be just fine." A small object on the floor caught his attention; he leaned forward to pick it up. He held it between his fingertips, studying it for a moment. "You don't think Rob was sleepwalking, do you, Troy?" He placed the object into his shirt pocket.

"No, sir. I guess not."

"Why not?" Carl asked.

"Well, you should have seen how he looked at me." Carl sensed Troy getting worked up and didn't want to push the boy any further. Still, he needed answers.

"How did he look at you, son?"

Troy searched for the exact words to say and shifted his eyes to the floor.

"Just between you and me, Troy. It might help your friend," Carl assured him.

Troy finally spit it out. "He looked at me like ... like he was hungry."

Carl thanked Donald and Lois for the coffee and then shook Troy's hand. "Thank you for showing me around the Scream in the Dark. I wish I'd been here to see it in action." He placed his hat on his head and straightened it out.

"I would appreciate it if you could do what I asked," he told Lois and Don. "I'll call you tonight and let you know what's up."

"Sure, Sheriff," Don said, then shook his hand. "If there's anything else ... you know. And if you see Karin and Bob, tell them not to hesitate, whatever it is."

"Will do," he replied. "Thanks again; sorry to bother you on a Sunday." He nodded to Lois.

"Good to see you, Carl." She smiled.

Sheriff Primrose climbed into his cruiser and turned the engine over. He waved to the Fischer family where they stood on the front porch. Then he reached into his front pocket and pulled out the small object he had found on the garage floor. He turned it over in his hand. A giant knot grew deep inside him as he studied it.

It was a human molar with dried blood covering the root. Carl had a good idea the tooth belonged to Robert Boyle. The child had likely lost it while convulsing.

He hadn't shared the discovery with Don or Lois, and he sure as hell wasn't about to tell Troy. Carl felt sick to his stomach. This wasn't good at all, and it sure didn't sound like the flu. He prayed Dr. Malcolm would figure this out soon. Carl had enough on his own plate. There was an ongoing murder investigation with no defined cause of death, and he needed to get in touch with Burt as soon as possible.

Static from the police band broke the silence. "Base to Sheriff Primrose. Are you there, Sheriff? Over."

The knot in Carl's stomach tightened like a noose around his neck. The tone in Tara's voice told him she wasn't calling with good news. He picked up the handset and paused. For the fortieth time today, he asked himself, *"What the hell is going on around here?"*

CHAPTER 9

The medical examiner's office was located on the Boulevard near the Chilton Medical Center. The front part of the brick-faced building housed a small reception area and an even smaller office where Burt kept his files, a desk, and a hidden bottle of booze. The rear of the building held the morgue, the laboratory, and "Old Smokey" the incinerator. This was where all the heavy lifting was done. Burt opened the back door, stepping out of the harsh stainless steel coldness of the morgue, just as the meat wagon pulled into the secluded parking area behind the building.

Burt Lively had served as the King County medical examiner for longer than even he could remember. During those years, he had witnessed far too many senseless deaths. The morgue was usually filled with a mix of natural causes, automobile fatalities, and the occasional hunting accident. There had only been a few instances of the latter, but they had stuck out in Burt's mind. Once, a forty-five-year-old man had ventured out at the start of buck season but neglected to clean his 12 gauge before leaving the house that morning. A field mouse had found its way into the barrel of the man's Mossberg and built a nest over the winter. With several hours to go before sunrise, the guy parked himself in his tree stand and waited for a hefty 8-pointer to pass. Whatever did walk by had had a lot more luck than that poor bastard did. The guy grabbed his shotgun and fired at what he thought would be the talk of the lodge. Instead of discharging a slug into the heart of the animal, the barrel exploded in the man's hands and blew half of his face off. What a mess.

Another hunting-related death that stuck out in Burt's mind happened in '73 when a massive blizzard crippled the entire state for a week and a half. A second hunter, with an equal amount of luck, had gone out just before the snow started falling. He must have gotten disoriented in the whiteout and been unable to navigate his way through the forest. Park rangers found him weeks later after the bulk of the snow melted. By then, damn near every creature on the mountain had taken a bite out of the guy. But King County usually wasn't that exciting, and they'd never seen anything close to what the sheriff's department found on Foothills Drive early this morning.

Burt walked back into the morgue, opened the icebox, and pulled out the long retractable shelf. He went to his office to check his answering machine and waited for his guys to transfer the body to the freezer slab. There were no messages, not that he expected there to be. He told Deputy Forsyth there was no rush and imagined he wouldn't hear anything until later in the day. He returned to the morgue to meet Abe and Tony as they wheeled the gurney through the back entrance. The men positioned it next to the slab and unzipped the black body bag. Then, they transferred Felix Castillo onto the cold steel of the freezer shelf. Abe started to push it back in when Burt stopped him.

"Don't worry about that, Abe," Burt told his driver. "I want to check on a couple things first."

"No problem," Abe answered. "Is there anything else we can do before we head out?"

"No, I've got it from here. Sorry to call you guys in on a Sunday morning. Thanks for your help." Burt had already begun to examine the corpse and barely noticed when Abe and Tony walked out the back door and closed it behind them.

The old coroner pulled on a fresh set of gloves, then positioned a sizeable fluorescent light with a retractable arm directly over the body to help his tired eyes. Stark white light illuminated the corpse, arresting every shadow in the room. The light revealed the victim's face, and Burt did a double take. Felix Castillo's cheeks appeared flush with color, which seemed more than a little off.

This morning they had been a pale shade of blue, the hue you would expect to find on a dead body that had been left outside in the cold or one devoid of body fluids. Now his cheeks were almost pink, and he looked as if he couldn't have been dead for longer than an hour, two at the most.

Burt checked the wound and recoiled with a start, quickly removing his hands as if he had touched a flame. "What on Earth?" he gasped, then slowly returned his fingertips to the man's neck. Felix Castillo had been ice cold less than three hours ago when Burt examined him on the street. Now the man's skin felt closer to seventy-five or eighty degrees, maybe even higher.

"What the hell is going on?" he whispered to the empty room.

The phone rang, causing Burt to jump. "Oh, Jesus Christ, Burt. Get a grip, will ya?" He moved to turn off the light, then thought better of it and left the morgue to answer the phone.

"This is Burt," he said.

"Hi, Burt, it's Gary. I've got some info, but there isn't a whole heck of a lot I could find out." Deputy Forsyth paused.

Burt sat at his desk and took out a notepad and pen. "Okay, what have you got?"

"Well, as we already knew from his ID, his name's Felix Castillo, age twenty-nine, from Warren. He worked for Con Ed for the past nine years, no next of kin."

"None?" Burt asked.

"Zero; no parents, no wife, and no kids."

"Jeez, poor bastard. That's even sadder than dying in the middle of the street."

"If you say so, Burt." Gary cleared his throat. "No medical conditions, no arrest records. His boss said he was a model employee. Worked as much overtime as you could throw at him."

"I guess that would explain why he had no wife," Burt added.

"If you say so, Burt," the deputy repeated.

The back door of the morgue suddenly slammed. Burt looked up from his notes. "Is that you, Abe?" he called. There was no response.

"Are you there, Burt?" Gary asked.

"Huh, yeah, hold on one second, will ya?" Burt covered the receiver with his palm and called out, "Hey, Abe. What's going on back there?"

Burt waited for Abe to answer but only heard the motor of the freezer. "Hey, Gary, let me call you back in a minute."

"You got it, Burt." The deputy hung up.

Burt put the receiver back on the cradle and entered the hallway. "Abe," he called as he walked towards the examination area. "I told you I was good here. No need to hang around any longer."

He rounded the corner. "Abe, what are you de—" Burt stopped short in the entranceway. "Jumping Jesus Christ!" He stared in disbelief. The room was silent; Abe had not entered through the back door and neither had

Tony. The area was completely empty. The freezer shelf was exactly where Burt had left it, except Felix Castillo's body was no longer on it.

Burt ran to the back door and burst into the parking lot. It was empty as well; no Abe, no Tony, and no Felix Castillo. His mind raced to draw a logical conclusion but was unable to. Every possible scenario ran back to an impossible dead end. He had never lost a corpse before and had no idea what the protocol was for such an occurrence. Someone had to have come in the back door and stolen it. He thought about the call he needed to make. Carl was going to blow a gasket. This was bad. *Jesus Christ, this is so very, very bad.*

"What in the name of all things holy?" Burt asked the empty parking lot. The sound of the wind was his only reply.

Dr. Ethan Ziegler had been running on fumes for the past six hours and been at the center going on eighteen. He checked his watch to confirm. His back ached, his head throbbed, and the coffee from the cafeteria sat in his gut like a rock. Dr. Malcolm had been ready to quarantine Chilton's east wing and the emergency room staff, as well as Sheriff Primrose and one of his deputies. But Ziegler managed to convince him otherwise, mostly because he didn't want to get stuck there himself, which is exactly what happened. And Malcolm left him in charge of the whole shooting match. A grocery list of tests needed to be executed and evaluated, from x-rays to blood work with a full tox screen, even urinalysis. Sadly, he wasn't any closer to diagnosing the children than he had been when they were first admitted. He needed answers by six tomorrow morning, or Dr. Malcolm was going to pull the plug and call in the quarantine. *If it comes to that, I'll have much bigger problems to deal with.*

He swallowed the last gulp of his coffee, got up from his desk, and made his way to the lab.

"Good morning, Dr. Ziegler." A young candy striper with shoulder-length blonde hair passed him, pushing a cart of books and stuffed animals. She wore a pink and white uniform that hugged her figure, making her look like an hourglass-shaped peppermint stick.

He nodded to the girl, and on any other day, he would have stopped and chatted her up, but there was no time for that. Ziegler opened the door to the lab and barged in on a heavy-set man with a thick black mustache who looked up when he entered the cluttered lab.

Peter Gillick, the lab tech, worked for the center long before Dr. Ziegler had been hired. He was a big man, and not just tall either. Peter stood well over six-four and looked like he hadn't missed a meal during his entire career. His massive figure engulfed the microscope in front of him like a water buffalo sipping from a shot glass.

"Hey, Doc." Peter nodded.

"Peter. Got anything?"

The big man winced and tightened his enormous lips. "You realize blood work takes time? Not to mention it's Sunday, and I'm the only one here." Peter shifted on a stool that creaked in protest under the strain. "By the way, I'm good. Thanks for asking."

"I'm sorry, Peter," Ziegler offered. "It's been a hell of a day. I was hoping you had something. I guess not."

"Well, I didn't say that. It'll still be a few hours before the rest of the results are in, but I did find something interesting."

Ziegler raised his head and took a lunging step forward. "So, you got something?"

"Take a look at this, Doc." Peter backed away from the table, allowing Ziegler to look into the microscope.

"This is a sample from Erin Richards," Peter explained as the doctor examined the slide. "As you can see, there isn't any sign of a viral agent present. However, there is an elevated concentration of white cells, indicating an infection. But—"

"Am I seeing this right?" Ziegler asked and raised his head.

"I was asking myself the same thing when you walked into the room."

"Poison?" Dr. Ziegler looked back into the microscope. "I mean, is that what I'm seeing? It looks like these kids have been poisoned."

"Yeah, I think so. Except this isn't like any poison I've ever seen. And I'm still not entirely convinced that's the only thing going on here. There is a bacterial signature you can see that has attacked the red blood cells. It behaves much like a parasite, attaching itself and feeding, almost like a tick."

"Is it the same in all three children?"

"Identical," Peter answered.

"Then they all came in contact with the same toxin. If that's even what it is," Ziegler said more to himself. "A bacterial parasite of some variety."

The sample taken from Erin Richards clearly revealed a foreign agent. The infection had compromised the integrity of the plasma, causing her blood proteins to denature. In an attempt to fight off the infection, the girl's immune system kicked her white blood cells into overdrive. They had begun to destroy the red cells where the toxin was centralized. Her body was eating itself.

"They're not going to last much longer unless we figure out exactly what the hell this thing is." Ziegler felt the icy fingers of time tightening around his throat. "I've never seen anything like this. What do you make of it?"

"At this point, Doc, I don't even want to guess. Toxicology will take another hour or so. We'll have a little more to go on when that's finished. I called in a couple of the other techs, and they should be here any minute." Peter checked his watch: eleven thirty.

"I don't know how much longer those poor kids can last."

"I know, Doc." Peter grabbed a pipette and a box of slides from the counter. "As soon as I have something, I'll call you. I'm doing everything I can."

"Thank you. Page me when you've got something." Ziegler walked out of the lab and sped off as fast as he had come.

The blood work confirmed the evidence of an infection, which was obvious from the high-grade fever. The agent attacking the children's red blood cells possessed the qualities of a poison. It also contained a biological signature, like that of a single-celled bacterium. It was unlike anything Ethan Ziegler had ever seen. Erin's body was feeding on itself in an attempt to fight off the foreign invader, one nasty bacteria or poison or whatever the hell it was. By the look of it, Ziegler believed it might be a hybrid of the two, if that was even possible. Up until a few minutes ago, he hadn't thought it was. But now, he wasn't so sure. He tore down the hall toward radiology and passed the same blonde candy striper from before. She smiled at him and probably batted her eyes, but Ziegler didn't even notice.

Robert Boyle lay in room 3 of the ICU wing. He had been placed on a ventilator early that morning after becoming unable to maintain his respiration. Sweat ran from every pore of the child's body, and he had lost nearly ten pounds since Thursday. His color was near that of a corpse—pallid, pale, and almost blue. Two of his teeth had popped out when the doctors inserted the breathing tube, and the rest had fallen out shortly after, as if his body was too weak to hold on to them. Nurse TenHove entered the room in a full-protective body gown with head gear.

His parents hadn't left the building since they arrived and had only been permitted to visit from no closer than the doorway. As a courtesy, the staff provided rooms for both families to wash up and rest. Dr. Ziegler prescribed the mothers a light sedative to help them relax ... if only slightly.

Nurse TenHove recorded Rob's vitals and checked his IV. She registered the stats in the boy's chart, then hung it back at the foot of the bed. Taking one last look at the child, she turned and left the room.

Robert Boyle opened his eyes and stared up at the ceiling. His dark pupils had consumed the irises, making his eyes as black as tar. A transparent film shuttered across them from side to side; a secondary eyelid much like an amphibian's had developed. It shielded out much of the bright fluorescent light, which was too painful to look at directly. Then Rob closed both sets of lids and lay there listening to the steady pump of the ventilator.

Carl stood in the morgue with his hands on his hips and a look on his face that a mother might give a child who repeatedly stuck pennies into the wall outlet. He'd gotten the call from Tara and known right away by the tone of her voice it was bad news. But he never could have imagined.

Burt stared back at him, even more puzzled and confused.

"Let me get this straight. You're telling me you *lost* the body?" Carl asked again.

"It was right here." Burt motioned to the freezer shelf with both hands. "I just started examining the guy when the phone rang. It was your deputy. Couldn't have been more than five minutes. Then I heard the door slam and figured Abe came back for some reason. But it locks from the inside. So, I thought maybe some kids were trying to break in or something.”

“And what about Abe and your other guy?” Carl searched for the man’s name.

“Tony,” Burt answered. “It wasn’t them. I called on the radio. Abe was parking the wagon in the lot at the medical center.”

“So, where’s the body, Burt?” Carl took off his hat and scratched his head. “Correct me if I’m wrong, but the guy didn’t walk out of here on his own. Please tell me that’s not what you’re suggesting.”

“Of course not!” Burt shouted. “What do you take me for, a goddamn fool? I know the guy didn’t walk out of here on his own, Carl. Somebody came in here and stole the body!”

Carl pursed his lips and replaced his hat on his head. “Okay,” he said. “We have a body snatcher in Garrett Grove. I’m sure you checked the rest of the drawers. Not to insult you, but I’m having a hard time swallowing any of this.”

“Goddamn it, Carl!” Burt stormed to the freezer in a huff and began to throw open the doors to prove he wasn’t entirely out of his mind. “Look, nothing here.” He opened one after the other, then slammed them shut. “Nothing in here either. I’m not crazy, Carl. Someone had to come in here and take the body.” He opened the last door revealing it, too, was empty. “Satisfied?”

“Not even a little. First, you tell me I should be on the lookout for a missing ten pints of blood, and now I need to issue an APB for the body that goes with it. I’m not very satisfied at all.” Carl examined the empty freezer shelf where the body had lain. The retractable fluorescent light still shone down onto the cold stainless steel.

“I know how this looks,” Burt said.

Carl stared at his friend. "Do you? How does it look, Burt?" He continued to inspect the shelf and the door to the freezer.

"It looks like I've lost my damn mind!"

"Yep, that's what it looks like." Carl was about to move the fluorescent light out of his way when he noticed something. He leaned in closer and then fished a plastic bag out of his pocket. "Hey, Burt, take a look at this."

The coroner walked over to the shelf to see what the sheriff was looking at. Caught in the retractable arm of the fluorescent light was a swatch of black hair. "Son of a bitch!" he exclaimed.

"Does that look like the color of the victim's to you?"

"Son of a bitch," Burt repeated.

Carl turned to him. "Dammit, Burt!" he snapped.

"Absolutely, dark black and coarse. The only guy in here with hair that dark in the past six months."

"Would I be correct in assuming that this light is cleaned regularly?" Carl waited for a reply.

"You would."

"And by the looks of it"—Carl mockingly gestured toward the large amount of grey on his friend's head——"this hair doesn't belong to you."

"Obviously." Burt rolled his eyes.

"Let me ask you something else, Burt." Carl studied the position of the light and the patch of hair caught in the hinge of the arm. "Has this light moved since you left the body and went in the office to answer the phone?"

The coroner thought about it for a second. "Nope, that's exactly where I left it. Yeah, right where I left it."

"Are you sure you didn't move this light?"

"I didn't move the damn light, Carl. It's in the same exact place I left it," Burt insisted.

Carl took a step back to view the examination shelf from a different angle, then approached it again and intently studied the patch of hair in the hinge. "You'd say the guy was about a buck-eighty, give or take?" Carl asked.

"Yeah, give or take, sounds about right," Burt replied.

"Took two guys to lift him onto the table; I imagine it would take two guys to carry him out as well. Would you agree?"

"Yeah, two guys, sure. He's dead weight. You know how hard it is to move a body."

"Burt, do you think two guys could lift Castillo off the table and carry him out the door without moving the light? I mean, they would have had to move the light, right?"

Burt studied how close the light was to the shelf and scratched his head. "Son of a bitch! You're right. I don't get it."

"What do you make of that?" Carl took a penlight out of his holster and illuminated the patch of hair. "Is that a piece of the guy's scalp?"

Burt looked closely. There was a decent-sized piece of scalp attached to the hair. Carl pulled it free with a pair of tweezers and dropped the evidence into the plastic bag. He handed the bag to Burt and took his hat off. "Could you hold these for a second?"

Before the old man could ask him what he was doing, Carl climbed onto the shelf and lay down in the position the body had been. He took extra caution not to disturb the position of the light. "Is this the way the body was laying?" he asked.

"Are you nuts, Carl?" Burt studied his friend with concern. "Yeah, that's how he was laying, but you're out of your damn mind."

Carl slowly sat up from his prone position; he lifted the top part of his torso until the tip of his head was an inch away from the light. If he allowed himself to sit completely upright, he would hit his scalp on the hinge, exactly where the patch of hair had been.

"You got to be shitting me." Burt's jaw dropped as he watched Carl's head graze the hinge exactly where Castillo's would, if he had …

Carl and Burt stared at each other. Neither said a word.

CHAPTER 10

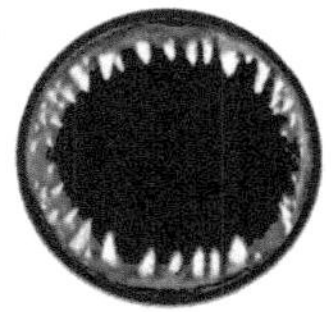

Butchie Post flipped the Spam over in the cast iron skillet and was greeted by a waft of sizzling goodness. The kitchen was poorly lit in the house he shared with his mother, Margaret, the same house he had grown up in, and the one he had come back to when his time at Barre Oaks had been paid in full. The old ranch wasn't much to look at. It needed a paint job, the gutters were overflowing with pine needles, and the yard was in serious need of attention. The place was structurally sound, but the interior was dank with the reek of stale cigarettes, as if the windows hadn't been opened since Kennedy was in office. The wallpaper was a musty shade of sour, the carpet smelled like a wet sock, and it wouldn't hurt if someone had taken the time to throw out the stacks of old newspapers and magazines that had taken over like an infestation.

Margaret had never been the happy homemaker type, and Butchie was ... well ... Butchie. After her husband left, Margaret did her best to raise her son, but it had been an uphill battle. The boy was a handful. She'd been in and out of the principal's office regularly in a futile attempt to keep the kid in school. And Butchie hadn't made it easy. When he was finally kicked out and sent to Barre Oaks, her two gins a night turned into three and then four. It wasn't long before she needed a couple shots in the morning just to steady the old nerves. Not like it was a problem or anything. Who didn't need a drink or two every now and then? Besides, the house was paid for, and she had her disability. Butchie had come home and gotten a decent job at the quarry. So, it wasn't like she was taking food out of their mouths to buy booze.

Margaret loved her son, and Butchie loved his momma. He flipped the Spam over in the pan one last time. Nice and crispy, just how she liked it. He buttered a piece of toast and fixed her a plate, then brought the food to her in the living room, where she sat watching Abbott and Costello. The comedians were dressed in baseball uniforms and performing their "Who's on First" bit. Margaret laughed and took a long sip from her Gilby's and tonic. A Pall Mall sat perched between her fingers with a two-inch ash defiantly clinging to the end.

"Here you go, Momma." Butchie placed her meal on a folding tray that sat next to her recliner.

"You're such a good boy, Butchie. Give your momma a kiss." She raised a cheek to her son, who kissed it and smiled. Margaret laughed again at the men on the television while Butchie went back into the kitchen and grabbed the items he had picked up at the A&P.

Margaret had needed Spam, bread, and two packs of smokes. Butchie's requirements were equally as simple. He headed out the back door, stepping onto the porch, and looked out into the woods behind his house. This time of year, one could expect to see an occasional buck or doe eating acorns on any of the numerous paths that cut through the foothills. Once, Butchie even spotted a mountain lion that must have gotten brave and ventured from its den on Garrett Mountain. Today, the trails behind the

Post house were empty, and that was just the way Butchie liked it. He didn't need anybody disturbing him this afternoon. Butchie had a few things he needed to take care of before Halloween. He gazed at the old shed, set at the far edge of his property, and his mind went right to thoughts of Jackie Gilmartin in her white nurse's outfit. It was going to look good torn to shreds on the floor of the shed. Butchie felt himself getting excited just thinking about it. He shook it off; he had a job to do.

He set the two shopping bags on the picnic table and sat down on a moldy patio chair. From the first bag, he removed the two dozen Red Delicious apples he had bought for the trick-or-treaters. He'd taken great care to make sure each one was shiny and crimson, with not a blemish or a wormhole in the bunch. *The kids are gonna love these.* Based on Butchie's own awful eating habits, he should have known that no kid in his right mind wanted to get an apple for Halloween. Still, somehow, he thought it was a good idea. Butchie's vision was obscured by his dark intentions.

He removed a sewing kit from the second bag, an extra box of needles, a roll of paper towels, and a bottle of Ipecac. He remembered playing in the garage when he was either five or six, back when his mom still called him Marion. There had been a shelf full of cans and bottles with automotive solvents and household chemicals on it. He couldn't be sure if he had drunk from the bottle, but Margaret told him she had walked into the garage and found young Marion downing a bottle of brake fluid. She called the family doctor, who recommended she give the boy a shot of Ipecac. Fortunately, she had a bottle of the vile liquid in the house and forced fed several spoonfuls down her son's throat. At which point he vomited up the entire contents of his stomach and then some. He remembered that part, and even though he thought that he probably didn't drink the brake fluid, he never wanted to experience the Ipecac again. So, he learned his lesson about playing with bottles and stayed out of the garage.

Butchie sat in the early afternoon sun and got to work on his project. He set a large Tupperware bowl in the center of the table, removed the paper towels from the wrapper, and uncapped the Ipecac. The liquid smelled repulsive and brought back the traumatic childhood memory. Yet somehow, he managed to keep his breakfast down and continue.

He poured the medicine generously onto a handful of paper towels, then proceeded to rub the liquid over the skin of the apples. When he was finished with the first coat, he poured more of the medicine onto the fruit directly and let them sit in the Tupperware bowl to soak.

After he was satisfied that the apples had been sufficiently bathed in the Ipecac, he opened the sewing kit and the box of needles. Using the thimble, he began to push the tiny daggers into the apples. *Three needles per apple should do the trick.* Any dickweed kid who bit into one of these bad boys was sure to come away with a treat. If the little shits happened to miss the needles for some reason, the Ipecac would surely do the trick. Butchie thought better about his work and decided to insert a fourth needle into the pieces of fruit, pushing them in with the thimble far enough so they were undetectable.

He filled the bowl with the dangerous treats and, for good measure, poured the remainder of the liquid over them. He couldn't wait to hand these fuckers out to the neighborhood kids. *Trick-or-Treat my fat dick.*

The voice of a young boy broke the silence as well as Butchie's concentration. "Oh yeah, you and what army?" the kid shouted.

It was the two fartbags who had parked their bicycles next to Butchie's Monza earlier that morning. That had really pissed him off, but now the little dick lickers were riding on the paths just behind his house. He watched as they crested a small hill and disappeared into the woods.

"Oh no you don't, you little fuckwads. Not in my yard." Butchie jumped from his chair and bounded down the steps of the porch. He ran into the woods after the boys with blind rage coursing through his veins. They had a lot of nerve riding their bikes on his property.

The land between Mountain Ave and Foothills Drive was state property and open to the public, but Butchie didn't see it that way. Most of the time, kids were smart enough to avoid the section of the paths bordering the Post property, unless, of course, they were looking to get the ever-living shit kicked out of them. Tommy Negal and Jeff Campbell weren't the brightest kids in the fourth grade and hadn't realized they'd driven their bikes within earshot of the town lunatic. It was a mistake neither of them would regret for long.

Ziegler stood before the back-lit panel, staring at the impossible images in front of him. It had to be some type of mistake; surely there was something wrong with the equipment. It happened. That was the problem with technology; it wasn't foolproof. Even the most advanced systems showed faulty readings from time to time. But there had been no mistake, and what he was looking at wasn't the result of faulty equipment or inaccurate readings.

He'd ordered chest x-rays to be taken of the children in the ICU, and all the images had come back the same. The techs in radiology had been so startled by the initial results, they'd taken a second set of photos. Which hadn't been easy with the Boyle kid on a ventilator. Now, looking at the results, Ziegler imagined it wouldn't be long before the Richards kids were on ventilators as well.

Both the first and second sets of x-rays revealed the same thing. The children's internal physiology had been altered. The lung capacity of the children had decreased by nearly thirty percent. Not just their ability to take in and process air, but the actual size of their lungs had been reduced. It was as if their bodies were being subjected to the effects of extreme pressure. And that wasn't even the most startling abnormality the photos revealed. The children's hearts had increased in size and were nearly twice as big as a ten-year-old's should be. It was impossible, but the x-rays didn't lie. The proof was sitting in front of him.

There wasn't a germ on the planet capable of that. Ziegler was in way over his head and knew he had made a horrible mistake by convincing Dr. Malcolm to change his mind about the quarantine. It was a race against time to find an answer that might save these children. And Ethan Ziegler was losing confidence in his ability to do that. Not to mention the growing probability that through his hubris, he had released an unidentified contagion back into the populace of Garrett Grove.

Fuck ... Malcolm was right ... this is all my fucking fault!

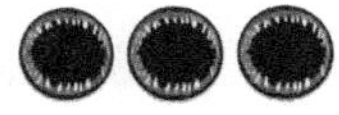

It waited ... watching ... listening ... ready to feed. It heard the echoes and felt the ground move from behind the walls of its prison. Then the rock shifted, and light swarmed the darkness. Free at last. It had been tricked by the simple creatures it once controlled and fed on. They had lured it into the shadows and trapped it with their magic. But they would pay. It rushed from the cave, thirsting and famished, ready to exact revenge upon the ones. But the creatures were different. The worshipers of the Great Spirit, the ones who prayed to Ketanëtuwit, were no more. A new race had emerged, evolved over time. The new creatures had built machines to bend the will of the environment. They were fascinating. It sensed the heightened consciousness and intellect immediately; their thoughts were deafening, and the capacity of their emotions was limitless.

But it was vulnerable in its present state and needed to find a den. It didn't dare risk exposing itself, even though it was famished. It had been too long since it last fed.

Still, it understood restraint, which it had exercised with the younglings, draining its reserve even more. When it finally consumed, it had been ravenous. The emotions of this new race were like nothing it had ever ingested. Their desires had evolved, their emotions were refined, and their fear was glorious. Their nourishment was deliciously intoxicating. It had been driven to a frenzy by the salacious thoughts of the one called Felix and drained the vessel dry, an unavoidable mistake. Now, there was great work to be done once again. Vessels to be drained, consciousness to be absorbed, and innocence to be devoured. Nothing satiated its hunger like the innocence of the younglings. Their fear was exquisite.

Tommy and Jeff pretended their bicycles were X-wing fighters as they navigated the asteroid belt behind Butchie's house. They were presently mounting an attack on the Death Star.

"Red One to Gold Leader, he's on your tail, defensive maneuvers," Jeff yelled, with dust spitting from his back tire.

"Roger, Red One. I'm on it." Tommy hit the brakes and pretended to fire laser cannons at an enemy TIE fighter.

"Gold Leader, I have a shot. Cover me," Jeff shouted and pedaled faster towards his imaginary target.

"Copy that, Red One. Take your shot when you're ready." Tommy followed close behind. Loose sand took to the air as they tore through the trails that had been carved into the woods so long ago.

It watched the young ones from where it hid. The creatures passed within feet of where it waited and never noticed it. They had evolved in many ways but had lost their primordial instincts; they could no longer sense the threat of a predator. It followed unseen, like a vapor.

"I'm taking the shot, Gold Leader." Jeff fired his cannons at the Death Star. "Direct hit, let's get out of here before she blows."

Closer ...

The boys followed the path to the right, around a large oak tree, and headed in the direction of the creek. The trail took a slow downgrade, their tires bouncing over ruts in the dirt formed by heavy rains. The woods grew darker around them as they drew closer to the small stream.

Closer ...

Tommy and Jeff were feeling pretty psyched about blowing up the Death Star. Jeff imagined being kissed by Princess Leia as she hung the medal of bravery around his neck. He turned back to yell at Tommy but was suddenly lifted from the seat of his bicycle. For a full second, he was aware of the feeling of weightlessness ... then, there was nothing but *Darkness.*

Tommy had about a half a second longer than Jeff to register what was happening. He watched as his friend was lifted from the seat of the bicycle in front of him. It seized Tommy and held him by the throat, making it impossible for the boy to breathe. Tommy opened his mouth to scream as his eyes rolled back into his head. But by then, it was over.

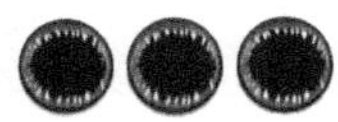

Butchie saw the two little rump rangers riding their bikes on his property and had run after them. The pricks were yelling and screaming like they owned the place. But this was his yard, and he was about to teach them a lesson they weren't soon to forget. He heard them calling each other things like red and gold and imagined it was some type of code for sissies. Butchie knew these trails better than anybody. He ought to; they were his. The queer baits were headed toward the creek, and the trail was a dead end. Butchie cut into the woods; willows slapped at his face and stung like tiny wasps. It was familiar ground, not far from where he had finally stood up for himself all those years ago. And he was about to stand up again. He could feel his excitement growing at the thought of confronting the little pussies. He thought he might even show them a little trick he had learned in Barre Oaks.

The boys had stopped yelling. Butchie listened as he approached the creek. Taking a running leap, he cleared the little brook and landed on the opposite bank. He continued to run, never missing a step. Butchie exited the woods and emerged onto the path. The little humps would be just around the next corner. The air in his lungs began to burn; he had worked up a sweat, not to mention he could feel the heat in his balls growing hotter by the second. He bounded up the trail and turned the corner.

Butchie stopped short in his tracks.

The kids' bicycles lay in a tangle where they had come to rest half on and half off the path. The back tire of one still spun mindlessly. Butchie thought he must be seeing things; some type of trick or illusion of light played with his vision. He attempted to register what he saw but was unable.

The two kids hung in the air about three feet above the ground; their arms and legs dangled from their motionless bodies. Butchie struggled to see if anything was tied around their necks; they looked as if they had been lynched. But there was nothing. The children simply floated before him, suspended by some invisible force. "What the f—"

He sensed the presence at once. It was easy for evil to recognize itself. Butchie was overcome with the urgency to run but found it impossible to move. He knew if he didn't react, he would never get another chance. He finally tried to turn, but it was too late. It rushed him like a gust of wind. Suddenly, it was in his mouth, entering through his eyes, and forcing itself into his ears. It violated every part of him. He was invaded like never before, nothing like the way he'd been taken in Barre Oaks. For a moment, Butchie felt it inside his head. Then it spoke, and he knew he had been chosen. He had only been chosen once before, by Vinnie and the Bristol Boys. It was good to be selected; it meant you were important. It meant you were a giver, not a taker.

Butchie was lifted off the ground as it entered him and revealed in detail the great work that was before him. His feet hung several feet above the dirt as it consumed him, and Marion "Butchie" Post ceased to exist.

CHAPTER 11

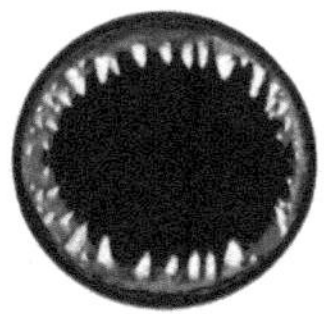

Wilson's Diner maintained a steady flow of customers throughout the week, then picked up considerably on Saturday and Sunday. Dick Wilson owned the place and could usually be found slinging burgers and deep-frying potatoes behind the grill. On the rare occasions when Dick wasn't there, his nephew Josh piloted the ship.

It was nothing more than your typical greasy spoon, but it was the only diner within a twenty-mile radius. Which was great for business but bad for the town's cholesterol. Today's lunch had been busy like most Sundays. Amanda Griggs, who everyone called Mandy, like the girl in the song, had worked the floor. Mandy was twenty-five and quite the looker, which kept the truckers and quarrymen coming back. Who didn't love a pretty face? She was good with the kids, friendly, courteous, and she knew how to flirt a fat tip out of every guy that walked into the joint. One of her favorite moves was to unbutton her blouse as far as gravity would allow, then lean over the counter to offer the truckers and quarrymen an eyeful. The girl sold more peach cobbler than any other waitress who worked there, and

Dick had seen how she did it. In fact, Dick was thinking about moving the chicken liver to the top shelf just to see how much of the disgusting paste Mandy could peddle by standing on her tiptoes and showing off her ass cheeks. Dick was willing to bet he'd have a hard time keeping it in stock.

When lunch was over, only a few customers remained. A family of three sat at a table near the window finishing their meal, two men from the quarry had just paid their bill, and Dr. Malcolm sat in the far booth, keeping to himself. The chief of medicine had started to visit the place a bit more frequently since his wife, Rosie, passed away two years prior. They were married nearly forty years. She had always been a big woman and had struggled with diabetes for a long time. But she lost the battle in the end.

Rose Malcolm doted over her husband for as long as she could. Right up until she became unable to make breakfast for him in the morning. Most people believed John would pass shortly after Rose. Married men usually didn't fare well after the death of their spouse.

So far, Dr. John Malcolm proved to be an exception to the rule. Most likely, it was the job that kept him vital. However, as the song goes, to everything there is a season. John knew he was getting a little long in the tooth and it was time to let the young bucks do some of the heavy lifting. So he hired Ethan Ziegler, a talented young surgeon and a damn good diagnostician. But John wasn't ready to be sent to the glue factory just yet. Although the hours were getting to him, he was concerned if he acquiesced to Mother Nature's call to leisure, it wouldn't be long before the girls at the beauty parlor were saying, "Poor old Dr. Malcolm, he just wasn't the same after his Rosie passed. He died of a broken heart".

Besides, plenty of patients in Garrett Grove preferred seeing the chief of medicine rather than young Dr. Ziegler. Some felt Ziegler was a bit too casual. Also, there was talk about his relationships with a few of the nurses.

That didn't necessarily make him a bad doctor, but it made some of the older population uncomfortable.

Jackie Gilmartin had been running the bases with Dr. Ziegler regularly and had shared their recent exploits with her roommate, Mandy Griggs. Jackie liked to stop by Wilson's after work for a bite to eat and a little conversation. The girls shared every detail about their sex lives, and Mandy loved hearing about the randy Dr. Ziegler, who had an excellent bedside manner.

That morning after work, Jackie told Mandy about her and Ziegler's plans for this evening. The girls had made a bit of a spectacle of themselves during the breakfast rush. Which was pretty much the case whenever they were together. It was impossible not to notice them, with Mandy hanging half out of her skirt and blouse, and Jackie in her skintight nurse's uniform.

In turn, Mandy shared all the spicy details about her date at the drive-in with Felix and told Jackie how she had used the old cobbler trick on him. Her attempts to get the electrician's attention were successful, and they had gone to see *The Amityville Horror* up in Warren.

"How was the movie?" Jackie had asked.

"So good," Mandy answered. "We watched it three times."

That's when the girls started to cackle like two mother hens, which raised the eyes of everyone in the place.

"Mandy, don't you have tables to serve?" Dick scolded from behind the grill.

She poured Jackie a fresh cup of coffee, then leaned over the counter and whispered, "I'll be right back. Dick's a little grouchy today."

"Maybe you should offer him a slice of cobbler." Jackie smirked, which resulted in another bout of uncontrollable giggles. After breakfast, Jackie went home to the apartment to rest up for her big date with Ziegler.

Mandy approached the far booth where Dr. Malcolm sat alone.

"Can I get you anything else, Doc?" she asked as he sipped at his coffee, reading the Sunday paper.

"Thank you, hon. I'm good for now." He covered his mouth as he spoke, as if he was concerned that he might have food in his teeth. Although Mandy didn't realize it, Dr. Malcolm had chosen the far booth to avoid contact with the public.

Mandy set a stack of plates at the sink where Roger was busy scraping and washing. He was still in high school and worked as the busboy/dishwasher on weekends and after school. He was a cute kid, and Mandy liked to tease him a bit. Nothing serious, just enough to get him flustered and make him blush. She messed up his hair as she walked towards the back door, making sure to brush her hip against him as she did.

"Hey, Dick. I'm gonna take five out back," she called to her boss.

"Take the garbage with you," he barked.

Mandy rolled her eyes and grabbed the garbage can near the sink where Roger worked. She bent over far enough to give him a good look down the front of her blouse. She met his eyes as he scanned her rack. "See anything you like?"

He blushed as Mandy took the garbage and left out the back door. She stepped outside into the bright afternoon sunshine. It had been a warm October, but Mandy could tell the temperature was about to start dropping. Leaves had already begun to change colors on the oaks and the maples in town. And Garrett Mountain was starting to show large swatches of orange and burgundy on the north side.

The area behind Wilson's was a small lot the restaurant shared with Goldie's Beauty Parlor. Both businesses used it for deliveries, and it was where the garbage dumpsters were kept. A breeze whipped across the short stretch of blacktop, churning leaves into a mini cyclone in the center of the pavement. Mandy shivered as the cool air hit her bare legs and arms; it was going to be an early winter. There would be snow on the ground this time next month.

Mandy carried the garbage to the bin.

"Meow." A ginger-striped alley cat milled around the dumpster, looking for a free meal.

"Hey, Scraps," Mandy called to it. She had been feeding table scraps to the cat for several weeks and had aptly named it. She bent down to pet it. "How are you today, cutie?"

Scraps raised its head to be scratched more efficiently.

"Are you hungry?" she asked, removing a half of a turkey sandwich wrapped in tin foil from her apron. She set it down in front of Scraps, who tore into the offering like it was filet mignon.

The wind blew through the back lot again, kicking up an old newspaper and sending it wafting on the breeze. The rattle it made as it cartwheeled across the pavement spooked the cat, and Scraps retreated under the dumpster.

Mandy looked over her shoulder at the back door of the diner and the small alley separating the two businesses. A man stood in the shadows of the buildings; she had not noticed him until now. She drew in a sharp breath at the sudden sight and then relaxed when she recognized the familiar Con Ed uniform.

"Felix, what are you doing here?" she called to him.

He stood near the far wall, then stepped back and disappeared into the alley.

Scraps inched his head from beneath the dumpster and hissed. Mandy stood up and straightened her skirt. She and Felix had had a wild night at the drive-in, and she'd been looking forward to the next time they could see each other. They did it in the backseat of his car as the Lutz family battled the forces of evil on the big screen. It was obvious Felix had enjoyed it just as much, and even joked about meeting her behind the diner one day for a little afternoon delight. She had no idea he was serious.

Mandy had laughed it off but had secretly been aroused by the proposal. When Felix didn't come in this morning at his usual time, she thought he had used her. But he was here now. She couldn't believe he had actually picked today to surprise her. She found it incredibly exciting.

"I don't have enough time, baby," she called to him. "Dick only gave me a few minutes to take out the trash."

Mandy went to where Felix had been and peered down the alley. He had walked to the end and was standing with his back to her. *Cat and mouse, hmmm. This guy knows just how I like it.* She followed him down the alley.

"Baby, I don't have time today. Dick is expecting me back any minute," she explained. Still, she knew if he tried, she would let him have her. But that didn't mean she had to make it easy on him; she had to play a little hard to get. Mandy cursed herself for having worn her granny panties to work today but hoped Felix wouldn't mind too much.

Felix stared at the wall with his shoulders slumped and his back to her. There was something stimulating about the game he had initiated. Mandy could feel herself getting worked up as she approached him.

"Felix, baby, what are you doing here?" she asked coyly. "I didn't think you were going to show up today." She walked up to where he stood and watched him sway to the left and right as if he were listening to music.

"Baby," she said and touched his shoulder.

Felix spun around like an uncoiled spring and grabbed her, his hand clamping around her throat. He held her tight and stopped the air from entering her lungs. At first, she thought it was part of the game and found it thrilling, then she saw his face.

Felix stared back at her through a pool of onyx; his eyes were completely black, like they'd been filled with Indian ink. The veins in his face had bulged and ruptured. They spread out beneath his eyes like scarlet spider webs, making him look like he had aged a hundred years overnight. His neck was black and bruised, and there was blood on his shirt collar. Mandy tried to scream as he lifted her off the ground by the throat. Then he pulled her closer and opened his mouth impossibly wide.

Dear God!

His breath smelled like rotting meat. Mandy gagged as his grip tightened even more.

She didn't have to think about it for long. Felix opened his mouth wider still, his lower jaw descended with a sickening clack as the bones unhinged and dislocated. With the speed of a serpent, he drew her in and smothered Mandy's face with his gaping maw. The world was blocked out when Felix's putrid lips slurped against her skin. As she began to lose consciousness, she felt it rush into her. It forced itself into her mouth and down her throat. She thought it was his tongue for a second, except it was cold and horrible and tasted like death. She gagged and convulsed as her feet dangled above the ground. Her skirt rode up above her thighs as it took her. When Felix was finished, he tossed her to the pavement. Mandy's last clear thought before the lights went out was, *Oh no, my granny panties are showing.*

CHAPTER 12

Billy and Eric had been unable to focus their attention on raking the yard for different reasons. Billy was determined to get back to the top of Mountain Ave to discover what had stalked them last night. And if they happened to run into it, he intended to put a full load of buckshot into the fucker. Eric, on the other hand, just wanted to get Billy off his back. He wasn't interested in returning to the sanatorium, and he damn sure didn't want to run into that thing again. He was only going because Billy was making him. And whether they found it or not, he planned to never go back there again. He prayed they wouldn't find anything.

The Tobin brothers beat on Mick Petrie's front door for nearly five minutes before their friend finally answered, looking like something that had been pulled out of a litter box.

"What's up?" Mick opened the door with dark circles etched beneath his eyes, as if he had just rolled out of bed.

"Whoa, you look like shit," Billy said. "Allison kept you up late, huh?"

"No, man, she left right after you dropped us off." He rubbed his eyes and yawned. "What time is it anyway?"

"Past noon. You just getting up now?" Eric asked.

Mick didn't answer. He squinted at the midday sun and winced.

"Get dressed," Billy said. "We're going back, and you're coming with us."

Mick looked at him the same way that Eric had. He held no desire to go back up the mountain and was about to stand his ground. But he knew it was pointless to argue with Billy. His friend had a severe big brother complex and was used to getting what he wanted. It didn't matter what anyone else said. It was Billy's way or the highway. He was a master at debating and could outlast anyone in an argument. Billy was relentless.

"Man, I just got out of bed, and besides, I feel like shit." Despite his complaining, however, Mick knew he wasn't getting out of it.

"Get dressed and stop acting like a little bitch." Billy pushed his way inside, and Eric followed. A long staircase led to the main floor of the house; wallpaper depicting Revolutionary War battle scenes stretched upward toward the high ceiling. "We have to go back up there to find that thing. I brought the 12 gauge and the twenty-two. We're going to put it down." Billy passed his friend and then stopped; his attention focused on a large red splotch on Mick's neck.

"What the hell is that?" Billy pointed.

Mick reached to touch his neck, but Billy prevented him before he could. "Don't touch it, man. That doesn't look good at all. You got poison oak or something."

"Oh shit," Mick said as he raced up the stairs and headed to the bathroom. "That's all I need right now."

"Where are your folks?" Eric called after him.

"They went to my aunt's house for the week. They won't be back till Friday." The light came on in the bathroom. "Oh, shit! I got fucking poison oak!"

"I told you," Billy shouted from the living room. "Use some calamine lotion and get dressed, for Christ's sake."

A minute later, Mick came out of the bathroom with calamine lotion drying on his neck. Eric walked up to him and checked out the rash, which had already begun to blister.

"Jeez, dude, shit looks nasty. That's a pretty bad case of poison oak, might even be sumac." Eric winced. "Bet it itches like a bear."

"Not really. I didn't even notice until dickhead said something."

"Good," Billy pressed. "Throw some clothes on, and let's get going. We'll wait for you in the car." Billy smacked Eric in the bicep as he headed to the front door. It was Eric's cue to follow and Mick's to get his ass in gear. Once again, Billy Tobin had gotten his way.

They filed out of Billy's Charger and stood in the dirt lot of Mountainside Park. Eric studied the sun, which was still high enough in the sky to relieve his apprehension, if only just a little.

"Okay, just to be clear," Eric said. "If we don't find anything, we're outta here. We ain't hanging around, we ain't getting sidetracked, and we ain't staying after dark … right?"

Billy opened the trunk and removed the shotgun and the rifle. "Stop being such a little bitch and take this." He handed the .22 to Eric.

"I want the twelve." Eric held out his hand.

"I don't think so. This thing will knock you on your ass. Here you go."

Eric reluctantly accepted the rifle and grabbed an extra box of bullets from the trunk.

Mick, who was distracted by the rash on his neck, carried the bottle of calamine with him and obsessively continued to reapply it.

"Okay, let's go," Billy said, shoving extra shells into the pockets of his jacket, and slammed the trunk. A minute later, they set off up the old road.

Autumn had begun to take root on Garrett Mountain. The grass that wove its way through the cracks in the old pavement had turned brown and withered since the summer. Overgrown trees, once trimmed back to the side embankments of the extension, crept in and overhung the road. A good fifty percent of their leaves had turned gold or changed over to a dark burnt umber. Scores of them now littered the broken asphalt. They rattled across the road, swept along on the breeze, sounding like maracas as they danced over the crumbled pavement.

The road leading to the sanatorium looked even worse during the day than it had at night. Giant ruts eroded by the heavy rains and ankle-breaking chunks of loose asphalt littered the entire way. Cracks as big as fists zigzagged like lightning bolts in every direction. In some areas, full trees pushed their way through the blacktop, forcing broken pieces of the road up around their trunks.

Billy, Eric, and Mick carefully navigated the dangerous obstacle course as they made their way up the steep side of Garrett Mountain. They neared the halfway point when Mick started freaking out. He began scratching at the rash on his neck like a mangy dog. "Son of a bitch!" he yelled. "This shit is driving me nuts." He pulled off his jacket, which must have been rubbing up against the poison oak rash, and dug into his neck with his fingernails.

"Easy, dude," Eric said. "You're gonna make it worse. You're scratching it raw."

"Relax, man," Billy tried to calm him. "Let me see that stuff." He took the bottle of lotion from Mick and examined his friend's neck.

"Man, you've really scratched the shit out of yourself." Mick's neck had turned deep red and swelled. The blisters were so pronounced around the perimeter of the rash, Billy thought they almost looked like scales, like something you might see on a fish.

"It's bad, isn't it?" Mick continued to squirm.

"Well, it isn't good, but I never heard of anyone dying of poison oak. Might be sumac. But I think you'll live."

"Gimme that stuff." Mick grabbed the lotion out of Billy's hand and poured it directly onto his neck. Which seemed to help, and he relaxed a bit. After a few more dabs of the liquid, he was ready to continue.

They passed the spot where they had been ambushed the night before. There wasn't any evidence from the encounter other than some freshly kicked up asphalt and the branch Susan had tripped over. Nothing seemed out of the ordinary, although there was hardly anything ordinary about the old deserted road to begin with.

They could see the crest of the hill from where they stood with the sun in front of them, big and bright and shining directly in their faces. Suddenly, a figure appeared at the top of the mountain. Large and intrusive, clearly a masculine presence.

The boys shielded their eyes to get a better look. But the man was completely bathed in the shadow of his silhouette as his figure eclipsed the sun.

"Who the fuck is that?" Eric's voice grew shrill.

"I got no fuckin' idea," Billy answered.

A gust of wind kicked up, rattling a throng of freshly fallen leaves across the boy's path.

"I don't like this, Bill. Let's get the hell out of here." Eric turned to him.

"What the fuck? It looks like that lunatic Butchie Post," Mick said. "Don't ya think?"

"Shit, I hope not," Eric said. "I'd rather run into the demon bird from Hell than that psychopath. Let's go."

But it was too late for that; Billy had already decided to instigate. "Hey, asshole!" Billy screamed at the man. "What the fuck are you doing?" Billy didn't give a shit who it was; he was holding a 12 gauge Mossberg with two in the barrel.

The man didn't reply. He stood there in silence, staring down at them from his vantage point. The figure lifted his arms to the sky with intention, making him look like a cross between Moses parting the Red Sea and an Old West revival showman summoning the rain.

"You got to be shitting me," Mick spat under his breath. "I'm sure that's him. Look at the hair."

Everyone in town knew Butchie Post and avoided the guy like the plague. He was more than dangerous; he was psychotic. Billy squinted to get a better look. The guy sure looked like he had a mullet just like that jerk-off Post did, but it was hard to tell with the sun in his eyes.

The man stood there with his arms raised above his head like a Broadway dancer, and then something happened. The area around his feet started to move. It looked like heat waves rising off the pavement. Only it wasn't nearly hot enough for that, and it felt as if the temperature had even dropped some in the past few minutes.

The asphalt continued to weave in strange hypnotic waves, making it difficult to focus on. Then the illusion spread outward and moved toward them down the mountain.

"Are you seeing this, guys?" Mick asked. "What the hell is going on?"

"I think we better get out of here." Eric held the .22 at the ready.

The road appeared to melt in front of them, twisting and buckling before their eyes. Then, whatever it was started to spread faster, and suddenly, they could hear it. At first, they thought it was the wind. But it grew louder, and the boys realized the sound was coming from the mountain itself. By the time the moving waves descended a third of the way toward their position, the boys could see what it was, and suddenly, the peculiar noise made sense. It wasn't the wind at all. It was a hiss. The road was hissing.

"Jesus Christ!" Billy screamed.

"Are you fucking kidding me?" Eric shouted.

Thousands of snakes covered the road, making their way towards them. The coiling and winding of their bodies had caused the pavement to appear as if it were moving. It had looked exactly like waves. But now the boys could see them clearly enough to make out the individual bodies. Eastern diamondbacks and timber rattlers slithered toward them, mixed with corals, kings, copperheads, cottonmouths, and a horde of other serpents.

The snakes gathered at the maniac's feet at the top of the road, where they entwined around his legs. Their hissing grew louder and more intense as they made their descent; the sound of their rattles and the scraping of their bodies against the blacktop was so loud it drowned out the wind.

Billy turned to the others. "I'm not seeing this, am I?"

"Let's get the fuck out of here!" Eric screamed, and finally, Billy agreed.

It looked like every snake in King County had been dispatched to intercept them. And as impossible as it was to accept, it looked like the lunatic at the top of the hill was controlling them, like he had summoned them with his arms stretched out to the heavens. But that was just too insane to be real.

Billy realized it had been a horrible idea to come back. There was something terribly wrong with Garrett Mountain. "Yeah," Billy cried. "Let's get the fuck out of here!"

Both he and Eric turned to run, then realized Mick still hadn't moved. Eric went back for his friend and grabbed him by the arm, but Mick stood frozen in place, staring up at the man on the hill. Then he pivoted his head and focused on Eric with eyes that had turned solid black. The irises, the pupils, and the sclera looked like coal, as if they had fossilized.

"What the f-fuck, Mick? Are you okay?" Eric stammered, but his friend just stood there gawking at him with eyes as dark as the far side of the moon.

Mick's arms hung slack at his sides, and his bottom jaw hung open as if he were in a catatonic state. A thin line of saliva slipped off his lip and fell onto his shirt. From somewhere deep within his throat, it originated, a low, guttural growl like that of a bear or wolf. It happened so fast, Eric didn't see it coming. Mick lashed out and clamped onto his wrist with the speed and accuracy of a cat. Eric attempted to pull his hand free, but Mick held on with vice-like strength. An ear-splitting shriek echoed off the mountain like an air horn as Mick opened his mouth wider and threw his head back.

Despite how terrified he was and how every nerve in his body screamed at him to run, Eric was unable to move. He could only stand there, transfixed by the beckoning dark of the boy's eyes. It was impossible not to stare at them; they looked as if they were ... moving. The ink wells of Mick's eyes swelled and then pushed outward like they were about to pop from his head. They doubled in size to the point of bursting, and something inside them emerged. Eric watched in horror as a soot-like mist poured forth from Mick's black sockets.

The same strange substance lifted from his friend's open mouth and nostrils. It was dark and dense like the smoke from burning rubber. The cloud spiraled and churned in front of Mick's face as it flowed out of his orifices in a flood.

In a dizzying flash, the dark cloud propelled itself at Eric like a bullet. The boy's head was thrown backward as the toxic mass forced itself down his throat and into his nostrils. At first, he felt his insides freeze. Then his lungs began to burn as if they were on fire. A second later, Eric's shoulders slumped, and the cloud enveloped both of the boys.

Billy watched it happen, unable to say a word. He felt the piercing dagger of guilt slip between his ribs and penetrate his heart. *Eric, no! Don't let it touch you.* He wanted to run to his brother and pull him away from Mick but was too terrified to go near either one of them. *I'm sorry.* The cloud that swirled about their heads darted in furtive circles, making clear its ill intentions. And the first of the snakes had closed in on their position. A large cottonmouth wrapped itself around Eric's boot and coiled at his feet. It was joined by the approaching throng of serpents, which quickly gathered around the boys, attracted by the strange transfer.

Billy found himself drawn in by the swirling smoke, hypnotized by the tendrils that darted around Eric and Mick in a frenzy. Then he remembered he was holding a shotgun. He raised the Mossberg in the direction of the lunatic on the hill. *It has to be that fucking Post asshole.* And the army of serpents reacted in unison; the hoard of vipers raised their heads and struck out at him.

Billy prepared to fire, then felt the first snake dart across his sneaker. He looked down as a large copperhead slid across his foot and turned to strike. He jumped back, but they were everywhere; they covered the road, they wrapped around the other boys' feet, and they were on top of Billy as well. He backed away as even more emerged from the tree line behind Mick and his brother.

"Eric, wake up!" Billy pleaded. But Eric didn't move or was unable to hear him. The snakes pursued. He didn't realize he was crying as he stepped away from the army of reptiles that threatened to cut off his escape. Billy searched for an exit route down the mountain and found none. The serpents blocked the way; they had cornered him from nearly every direction.

Billy jumped when the large rattler struck. He was sure he had been hit, then realized it had only grazed his jeans. He retreated further from where Eric and Mick still stood with the strange smoke swirling about their heads like some demonic halo. Billy was forced back toward the tree line and further up the mountain. He jumped over the reptiles, but they continued to pursue him, separating him from his brother and friend.

The lunatic at the top of the mountain hadn't moved and was now covered in snakes. They hung from his arms and around his neck; they climbed his legs and blanketed the entire road. Again, Billy raised the 12 gauge, and the agitated throng of snakes shot toward him as if they knew his intentions. He turned and fired into the writhing mass of serpents. The buckshot scattered the snakes, but they were immediately replaced by hundreds more.

Eric and Mick turned toward him. The onyx cyclone increased in speed and changed direction. It focused on Billy with intention and purpose as another snake struck and nearly connected. He turned and fled into the woods, where it was considerably darker. Somehow the sun had already begun to set. *How long have I been here?* He ran blindly into the thick, and then he felt it. It bit down hard into his ankle, and Billy screamed. Then another one hit him on the leg; the pain was incredible. Billy fell to the forest floor screaming as dozens of sharp teeth ripped into his flesh.

CHAPTER 13

Father Kieran McCabe blessed himself before the altar in the Our Lady of the Mountain church. Walking below the vaulted ceiling, past rows of solid oak pews, he looked to his right at one of twelve stained glass windows that elaborately decorated the building's exterior walls. Refracted glints of crimson, blue, and gold were cast inward through images of Christ and his Passion on the cross, filling the entire church with a warm, welcoming glow.

Kieran had come to serve the parish exactly ten years ago in August. It was easy to recall because it had been the year of the massive traffic jam on the New York State Thruway. As he was making his way south to Garrett Grove, thousands of young adults were making their way north to a music festival intended to last all weekend long. And the traffic had been at a standstill. If that wasn't enough to make it memorable, the half-naked occupants of the minibuses and convertibles who had taken to flashing their whatnots at him as he passed certainly did. He recalled feeling embarrassed by their lack of modesty.

But that was ten years ago, and he'd been a different priest back then. Of course younger, just twenty-five at the time, but he'd been different in other ways as well. It was a strange time in the world. The war had been at full speed, and men he had grown up with were losing their lives in a country that no one had ever heard of until then. Kieran was only a few years out of seminary school at the time and been serving under Father Michael at Saint Benedict's.

Kieran had answered the call to the priesthood and never questioned the decision, nor had he ever felt that he missed out on anything by doing so. However, during the early years of his service, he lacked the confidence that only came with age and wisdom. He thought a great deal about the men who were risking their lives in Vietnam. The idea of so much death and suffering affected him on a spiritual level, and he came to believe his services might be better met as a chaplain in the armed forces.

Father Michael had listened to the young priest explain the sense of guilt he was experiencing. It didn't seem appropriate for there to be so much suffering while he lived contently, not when he was the one who had taken a vow to do the Lord's work.

"War is not the Lord's work, my son," Father Michael had told him.

"I realize that, Father. But I feel as though my services may be better utilized elsewhere."

Father Michael had been spiritually transitioning young priests for many years and seen nearly every crisis of faith imaginable. There had been similar pleas over a decade ago when men were sent into Korea. "Do you believe the Lord is calling you to the war in Vietnam?"

Kieran allowed the question to resonate. He didn't know for sure but thought it was possible. "I don't know, Father, but I think so."

"Father Kieran, you do realize you would be putting your own life in danger if you were to volunteer your services?"

"I understand, Father."

"I see." The old priest scratched his head and took a sip of wine. "You know you're not on this earth to end suffering? You're here to spread the word of our Lord, Jesus Christ." They both blessed themselves, making the sign of the cross on their foreheads and chests. "There are army chaplains who are trained to deal with what those men are going through. I think it is admirable you feel compelled to answer the call, but I don't see the logic in that path."

"Yes, Father." Kieran was disappointed, but he was not about to overstep his ground and risk angering Father Michael. "I appreciate your consideration in the matter, Father. It has weighed heavy on my heart for some time now."

"Yes, I can see that it has. But perhaps the answers you seek may be found elsewhere." Father Michael finished his glass of wine.

"I don't follow you, Father." Kieran said.

"I spoke with the archbishop earlier this week. There is a small parish in need of spiritual direction. Father Joseph Scott has suffered a heart attack and is not faring well. I believe you know Father Joe?"

"I do. I am so sorry to hear that, Father. Is he going to be all right?" Father Kieran asked.

"He is expected to recover, but it is unlikely that he will be fit to serve the parish in the same capacity."

"That's terrible. Father Joseph has done so much for the diocese. His presence will be sadly missed."

"I should think so." Father Michael poured himself another glass of the sacristy wine. He offered some to Kieran, who passed. The young priest had not yet acquired a taste for it.

"The archbishop is looking for someone to fill Father Joseph's shoes in Garrett Grove, and I believe this may be your calling. I couldn't think of anyone better suited for the job. Of course, I told His Excellence I would discuss it with you. He was concerned you may not be ready for the position, but I assured him you were."

Father Kieran was both embarrassed and flattered by his mentor's confidence in him. "Do you really believe I'm ready for my own parish, Father?"

"Well, my son, I think the real question is: do *you* believe you are ready for your own parish, or do you think you would be more useful in Vietnam?"

Father Kieran didn't have to think about it for long, and that had been the end of his spiritual crisis. He believed he wasn't doing enough, that he might be of better service as a chaplain in Vietnam. But Father Michael presented an alternative and thought Kieran might better service the Lord by leading his own parish. So, he accepted the position.

Father Kieran had made the trip from Utica to Garrett Grove the Thursday before Woodstock. Bumper-to-bumper traffic had shut down the northbound lanes on the thruway, and Kieran was practically the only one on the road traveling the opposite way. Girls with flowers in their hair hung out of the windows of their parked vehicles and waved to him. Some held up signs that read, *Make Love Not War*, and more than a few of the young ladies flashed him as he passed.

It embarrassed him to see the boldness of youth in all its glory exposed on the thruway. But it also filled him with a sense of affirmation. He had made the right decision. There was still work to be done here in America, just as there was work in Vietnam. Father Michael had chosen him for the position in Garrett Grove. A message was delivered in his time of crisis; it had been the work of the Lord.

Kieran watched the young souls stranded on the interstate and became convinced he had been chosen to help and pray for them. He was uplifted during that trip and offered a clearer image of the priest he was truly meant to be. A sense of direction swelled within him, and he felt his confidence grow. He experienced a spiritual awakening.

He wasn't the only one who had been given something that day. Many of those who made the trip to watch Janis Joplin, Crosby, Stills, Nash, and Young, and Jimi Hendrix took away a memory that had nothing to do with sex, or drugs, or rock-n-roll. The children of Woodstock returned home to tell their friends the story of the priest in the Chevy sedan who had honked his horn and given the peace sign to every girl that flashed him.

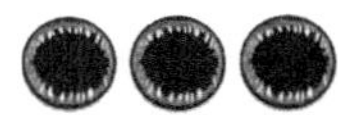

Sunday morning Mass had gone well, and Father Kieran shared the parable of the Good Samaritan. Our Lady of the Mountain held three services on Sunday: seven, ten, and noon. The ten o'clock service was typically the busiest of the three, with the seven a.m. being the warmup. Noon Mass was usually thin, but today had been slower than expected.

Still, Father Kieran did a fine job and faithfully delivered the message he had been called to do. He blew out the candles on either side of the entrance and exited the modest church through the stained glass front doors. He held his bible in his left hand, dipped the fingers of his right into the holy water, and made the sign of the cross. Allowing the door to swing closed behind him, he walked outside.

A strong breeze gusted, rattling the leaves of the maples in front of Our Lady of the Mountain. The church sat far back on a large piece of acreage situated between Sunset Road and Mountain Ave and had been aptly named for its position in the heart of the foothills of Garrett Mountain. Pines and cedars lined the parking lot, except for a few areas where trails had been cut into the terrain centuries ago. The church was built in the fifties, and the land had been cleared by contractors hired by the diocese. Father Kieran heard that the original builders found a small fortune worth of arrowheads and artifacts during the construction. And to this day, treasure fever still ran high. It was common to see children scouring the woods behind the church, hunting for a trophy they could show off to their friends.

He walked across the parking lot and headed to the rectory, thinking he might enjoy a nice glass of wine. Father Michael would have enjoyed one himself if he were still alive. But sadly, his old mentor passed away last year, peacefully in his sleep. Father Kieran had spoken at the funeral and delivered the eulogy.

As he ascended the steps of the rectory, he paused for a moment. Out of the corner of his eye, a movement in the woods captured his attention. Father Kieran turned in time to see what looked like a hulking shadow darting in and about the trees at the edge of the parking lot. It traveled quick and was hard to follow. It was too fast to be a man and far too big as well.

He stood on the steps of the rectory, waiting. Then it moved again. This time he saw it more clearly. It looked like smoke; it was dark, almost brownish black in color. It was hard to tell exactly how big it was, but judging by how high it stood against the trees, it appeared to be no less than fifteen feet tall. The strange shape darted behind the great pines, passing quickly through some of them. Kieran inhaled deeply and scoured the woods for any signs of fire. He didn't smell anything ... not that he thought he would. By the way it moved, Kieran didn't believe it was smoke at all.

His heart quickened at the sight, and a chill gripped the back of his head just behind the ears. Again, he watched the shadow as it paused for a moment, concealed behind a thatch of fir branches, and then shot into the open, only to disappear behind the next swatch of trees. There was something very wrong about it. There was purpose in the way the form traveled, an intelligence; nothing moved that way by accident. It appeared as if it were ... hunting.

It started out as nothing more than a tremble, just the faintest shake in the very tips of his fingers. But it quickly progressed. Kieran's hands began to move uncontrollably, and then the tremors spread up his arms and settled into his chest. Fear seized him like a glacier, as if he had been plunged into a bath of ice water. It wrapped around his heart and threatened to stop it where he stood. It was evil, and it was only a stone's throw from his doorstep.

He struggled to pull himself away from the incapacitating fear that gripped him. He made the sign of the cross with sweat-slicked fingers and began to pray. *"Yea, though I walk through the valley of the shadow of death, I will fear no evil."*

Father Kieran preached of such; he warned his parishioners about Satan and the fires of Hell. And although he knew every word of it to be true, he had never witnessed anything malevolent or supernatural. As a Catholic priest, he'd heard of numerous accounts and read even more documentations of possessions and manifestations, but he had never witnessed anything firsthand. Now, gazing upon the presence in the woods before him, he knew he finally had. *"By the power of God, cast into hell Satan and all the evil spirits who wander through the world seeking the ruin of souls. Amen."*

The shadowy figure passed through the forest with furtive intention, then disappeared. Father Kieran prayed as he watched it vanish. "Hail

Mary, full of grace," he said as he opened the door to the rectory and rushed inside. He locked it behind him, then proceeded directly to the table with the decanter of sacristy wine and poured himself a full glass. He swallowed it in two gulps and quickly poured himself a second one.

CHAPTER 14

Deputy Gary Forsyth drove north on Route 3. In another mile, he would reach the Gables Bridge, which spanned the Lenape River, one of only two routes in and out of Garrett Grove. He slowed the cruiser and turned into the front parking lot shared by Wilson's Diner and Goldie's Beauty Parlor. Only a few vehicles were in the lot. He recognized Dick's green Maverick and Dr. Malcolm's Caddy. The old doc had been hitting the diner regularly since his wife had passed away.

Gary was about to make the trek into Warren to look through Felix Castillo's locker at the Con Edison plant. He'd spoken to the man's supervisor and gotten the green light to interview a few of Castillo's coworkers and check his belongings. Warren was the Grove's closest metropolis, but it would still take over an hour to get there.

He entered the diner and saw the old doctor sitting in the corner. "Afternoon, Dr. Malcolm. How are you today?" The aroma of deep-fried potatoes and heart disease hung in the air like a lard-filled piñata.

The doc looked up from his paper and smiled. "Hello there, Deputy. Nice to see you."

Dick noticed the deputy and met him at the counter.

"Deputy Forsyth, what's the good word?" Dick smiled and greeted him.

"Hey, Dick." He nodded. "I was looking for a cup of that jet fuel you been peddling."

"Sounds good. Is that for here or to go?" Dick looked over his shoulder into the back and then lowered his voice. "Mandy's around here somewhere." He winked at the officer.

Gary returned the smile. "That's to go, but I'm tempted to stick around for a couple hours."

"Milk, no sugar, right?"

"You got it."

Dick made the coffee and checked the back again. "Hey, Roger, you want to see what's taking that girl so long? She took the garbage out over fifteen minutes ago."

Roger took his apron off, hung it up, and walked towards the back door, which opened before he got there. Mandy stumbled in, cradling her head in her hand. Her skirt had ridden up her thighs, and her hair was messed.

"What the hell happened to you?" Dick barked.

Mandy lowered her hand to reveal a bruise on her forehead and her lipstick smeared across her cheek.

"Jesus, Mandy." Roger hurried to her side as she nearly toppled off her high heels. He scooped her up and helped her out of the kitchen, into one of the booths. Deputy Forsyth and Dr. Malcolm witnessed the state of the young girl and rushed to her aid.

Dr. Malcolm pushed his way through the group, forgetting he had been trying to distance himself, and knelt beside her. He lifted Mandy's chin and looked into her eyes. She had a nasty scrape on her forehead, and judging by her lipstick, she looked like she had been smooching in the back lot. He held up three fingers in front of her.

"How many fingers am I holding up, dear?"

"Three. I'm fine, Doc. I must have slipped outside by the dumpster." She blinked a couple times. "Really, I'm fine."

Malcolm was unconvinced and continued to examine her eyes as if he wasn't exactly happy with what he saw.

"What the hell happened?" Dick leaned in. "You were out there for over fifteen minutes. You said you were coming right back. And look at you, your lipstick's all smeared."

Mandy blushed. "Oh, excuse me a second, just let me clean up a bit."

"I think you should sit down for a little while," Malcolm told her.

"I'm fine." She pushed her way through the crowd of men and headed to the ladies' room.

Deputy Forsyth remained quiet and took mental notes. Mandy looked like she had been roughed up a bit. He had questions but thought it might be better to ask them in private rather than in front of her boss and the doc. He sipped his coffee and then pulled out his wallet.

"What do I owe you for the coffee?" he asked.

"It's on me, Deputy," Dick replied.

"No chance." He took out a dollar and left it on the bar.

Dick leaned over and whispered to him. "I'll bet she was out there with that lineman guy."

"What guy would that be?"

"The guy that works for the power company," he answered.

Gary raised his eyebrows. "Really?"

"I don't know his name. Freddy or something. Comes in after his shift every morning to flirt with Mandy and eat cobbler. They've been hitting it off pretty good, if you ask me." Dick confided in the deputy.

Mandy exited the ladies' room a bit more put together. She had fixed her makeup, straightened her skirt, and was using a piece of toilet paper to blot the scrape on her forehead.

"So, what the hell happened out there, missy?" Dick asked.

Mandy sat at the counter next to the deputy as Dr. Malcolm studied her.

"It was that guy, wasn't it?" Dick asked. "He was back there, wasn't he?"

Mandy blushed. "Yeah, Felix stopped by, and we talked for a second, that's all."

Deputy Forsyth choked on his coffee and almost spit it across the counter.

"What the hell did he do to ya?" Dick raised his voice. "Did the bastard hit you?"

"No," Mandy answered. "Felix isn't like that. He stopped by to say hi. I kissed him, and then he left. I was petting Scraps, and I think the little kitty must have gotten under my feet and tripped me."

"I told you to stop feeding that fleabag!" Dick shouted.

"Scraps is a good kitty. He's just hungry."

"Does your boyfriend work for the power company, Mandy?" Gary spoke up.

"Yeah, do you know him, Felix Castillo? He's worked for them for like ten years now."

Forsyth stared at the girl with his mouth open. Had he heard right? "Your boyfriend is Felix Castillo, black hair, Italian, works for Con Ed?"

"I just said that. I guess you *do* know him?"

Forsyth got up from the stool. "You said he was just here. Felix Castillo was just here?" Gary Forsyth had been the first officer at the scene to find the body of Felix Castillo face up on the cold pavement at five thirty this morning. So, either Mandy was hallucinating or the entire Sheriff's department had made a colossal mistake. At this point, he wasn't sure which it was.

He walked through the kitchen toward the back door. "Out here?" he asked and stepped outside. It was a small lot with two garbage dumpsters and a small alley separating the diner from the beauty parlor. First, he checked the dumpsters and walked around them. A skittish, orange-colored cat mewed as he passed. Then Gary crossed the lot and entered the alley to find it empty as well. Convinced there was nothing to be found, he returned through the diner's back entrance.

Dr. Malcolm remained at Mandy's side and continued to examine her eyes. "I don't think you have a concussion, but it wouldn't hurt for you to stop by the center and let us take an x-ray of that pretty little head of yours."

"Thanks, Doc. I'll probably come by with Jackie a little later." Mandy smiled. "I think I just want to go back to the apartment and take a hot bath." Mandy and Jackie's place wasn't far, just about a mile back into town.

"I'm not so sure you should be driving, the way you stumbled in here like that," Dr. Malcolm asserted.

Deputy Forsyth was unsure how to proceed. Mandy had to be lying about Felix, and her story about tripping over the cat didn't sound right either. There was something strange going on, and Mandy Griggs was hiding something. That much he was sure of. Still, it was hard to believe she had anything to do with the death of Felix Castillo. The girl just didn't have it in her. But Gary liked the idea of solving the murder on his own. No doubt there would be a promotion in it for him if he pulled that off.

"I'll drive you home, Mandy," the deputy said. "I was just headed up—" he stopped. "You can pick your car up later if you're up to it."

She smiled at him. "Thank you, that's sweet. I guess you're right. I probably shouldn't drive."

"How long ago did Felix leave?" he asked.

"I'm not sure really, my head's still kinda fuzzy. We were only out there for a few minutes, then he left."

"If that creep laid one finger on you, I'll break his legs!" Dick barked again.

"Don't be silly, Dick. Felix is one of the nice ones. He just showed up to say hi, and I gave him a little kiss, that's all."

The deputy studied her as she spoke. There was nothing about her body language or anything he could see in her eyes to indicate she was lying. But the facts were the facts; Felix Castillo was dead, despite the yarn Mandy was spinning. If she was lying, she was damn good at it. Hopefully, he would learn more on the drive. If there was any way to get to the bottom of this, it was by going along with whatever game Mandy Griggs was playing. She would slip up and say something eventually. Gary was counting on it.

"Make sure you have Nurse Gilmartin keep an eye on you until we get that x-ray." Dr. Malcolm smiled. "Doctor's orders, okay?"

"Thank you, Dr. Malcolm. I'm sure I'll be fine." She stood up and wobbled a bit on her high heels. Deputy Forsyth grabbed her and helped her to the door.

"My hero," she said. "Thanks for the help, guys. Thanks, Dick; thanks, Doc; see ya later, Roger." The young dishwasher hadn't said a word. He simply watched as the older men swept in and took care of everything.

"I hope you feel better, Mandy," Roger finally said, but she had already walked out the front door.

"Real smooth, Romeo." Dick snarled at the boy. "Don't you have some pots to wash or something?"

"Yeah, boss." Roger slumped his head and went back to work.

Dr. Malcolm had been on duty for twelve hours before placing Dr. Ziegler in charge. He didn't want to leave but was running out of steam long before the Richards twins had arrived. At sixty-five, John Malcolm couldn't work the marathon shifts that he used to. He considered retirement a little more this year than he had the year before. But in the end, it had only been a consideration and not a thought he acted on. He wasn't ready to be put out to pasture quite yet; maybe he would feel differently next year.

As much as he hated to leave the medical center, he needed to refuel. A quick bite to eat at Wilson's and a couple hours of rest in his own bed, then he would rush right back and be good to go. That was the plan.

He pulled his Caddy into the driveway. He and Rosie had raised three boys in the house on Midland Ave; now they all had children of their own. John had eight grandchildren, and the two oldest were enrolled at Dartmouth, studying medicine.

Rosie, the love of John's life, had needed her insulin three times a day, and it became more complex as she got older. She'd never been the healthiest of eaters, which drove John nuts. He tried everything he could think of to get his wife to take her health seriously. He didn't keep junk food in the house and had filled the refrigerator with vegetables and healthy snacks. But he couldn't watch over her all day. He knew she was cheating on her diet by her glucose level; the strips didn't lie. He was a doctor, after all. Rosie had a sweet tooth, and eating made her happy. It killed John to feel he needed to deprive her the enjoyment. But if it was going to save her life, he was willing to be the bad guy.

Rosie didn't understand how serious her condition was and refused to listen to John's constant pleading. That was until her right foot had gone gangrene and needed to be amputated. She ended up losing all the toes and several inches of the foot. After that, her disease progressed rapidly, partially due to the challenges of the missing foot but also because Rosie had fallen into a horrible depression.

John divided his time between Rosie and work and even hired a nurse to care for his wife when he couldn't be there. But no matter what he did, it never felt like enough. It tore him apart to think that he wasn't doing everything he could for her. He often thought he might have saved her if he'd left the job and dedicated every waking hour to watching over her. But it was unlikely to have made a difference, and it wouldn't have been good for either of them. There was no saving Rose Malcolm by that point, and John needed the job at the medical center as much as he needed her.

After Rosie died, John immersed himself into work even more. It became his only way of dealing with the loss. He just wouldn't be John Malcolm if he didn't have Chilton. He was the chief of medicine, after all. It was as much a part of him as his white hair. And now he had a new protégée to groom and mold. Ethan Ziegler was talented, but without John's guidance, he was likely to get himself jammed up, one way or another. If the guy was lucky, he would only knock up one of the nurses. But there was always the potential he could mess up on a far grander scale. So, John decided to stick around, at least until he was confident Ziegler could handle things on his own.

Now, he was pretty sure that day had come. John admired the way Ziegler stood up to him about the quarantine. It'd been a good idea to wait twenty-four hours, which allowed John the time to think. There was a lot more involved than he initially considered. He would have crippled the sheriff's department, knocked out the ER staff, and very likely started a panic in Garrett Grove. He was still concerned about the children in the ICU and would be back at their bedsides as soon as he got a few hours' sleep himself. But Ziegler had been right: they needed more information to go on before they did anything, and he was confident the young doctor had things well in hand.

John entered his spacious home and immediately felt the emptiness; it had been like that since Rosie had passed. She possessed a personality that had filled the place. Now it was more than just empty; it was barren. His footfalls echoed off every harsh surface as he made his way up the stairs. John inhaled, certain he could still detect the fading scent of Rosie's perfume. Estee by Estee Lauder; it had been her favorite.

For months after her passing, the fragrance permeated the house. It helped him feel as if she was still there, like he wasn't alone. There had been just a dapple left at the bottom of the bottle, which John continued to spray on her pillow once a week. The flowery intoxication warmed the bedroom with memories of Rosie that waltzed throughout the entire house. It greeted him when he returned home from work, kept him company when he ate his dinners by himself, and filled his dreams with visions of his beautiful wife and the aroma of her sweet perfume, each pump lasting long enough to keep her memory lucid. Then, slowly, it would fade, little by little, till it was barely detectable in the air. At which point, John would remove the bottle from Rosie's nightstand, inspect how dangerously low the contents had become, and repeat the process. Another flowery spray onto the pillowcase where she once laid her head.

It had been over a year since John used up the very last of the perfume, and although he was certain he could still detect the fragrance in the air, it was more of a memory than actually there. Sadly, nothing in this world ever lasted forever, except for maybe memories themselves. John walked down the hall and placed his keys on the dresser. There was enough time for a few hours of sleep. He took off his shoes, laid on the bed, and stared at the ceiling. He hated coming home now that Rosie and the perfume were gone and couldn't bring himself to purchase another bottle. Something about that didn't feel right, almost like cheating. He let out a deep sigh and stretched his hand to the side of the bed where Rosie had slept and placed it on her pillow.

"I miss you, Rosie," he said to the empty room.

CHAPTER 15

Deputy Gary Forsyth drove Mandy Griggs back to the apartment she shared with Jackie Gilmartin. She sat in the passenger's seat of the cruiser as he made his way down Route 3, obeying the speed limit. It was against departmental protocol to allow occupants to sit up front, but Gary wanted Mandy to feel as comfortable as possible. After all, she'd been dating the guy they found dead this morning and had implicated herself at the diner. Mandy claimed to have been with Felix only moments before the deputy's arrival. Which made her either a witness, an accessory, or completely full of shit. Forsyth was still trying to figure out which one it was. He hoped she might slip up and reveal something but knew there was little chance if she believed he suspected her.

Could it be she's that good and she is completely playing me? He studied Mandy as she checked her makeup in the mirror.

There's no way. No one is that good of an actor.

Still, there was something off about the girl. If she was involved with the death of Felix Castillo, then she had to realize Gary was on to her by now. But she didn't appear nervous, not even a little bit. She was more than convincing.

What the hell are you hiding? Gary wanted to get on the horn with Sheriff Primrose and tell him what he had discovered but didn't dare. He had a better chance of uncovering the truth if he used a bit more discretion.

Mandy shifted in the seat, her skirt riding up her thighs, revealing an eyeful that Gary had a hard time not checking out.

"You say you tripped over the cat in the alley and that's when you bumped your head?" He tried to keep his eyes on the road and study her reactions at the same time.

She pressed her lips and reapplied some lipstick. "Yeah, I think so." She returned the passenger mirror to the up position. "I guess I hit my head pretty good because the whole thing is a little fuzzy right now. But I remember Scraps. I think I fed him today."

"Well, by the looks of it, you hit the pavement pretty hard. You're gonna have a bit of a knot, I'm afraid," he told her.

She looked at him. "Does it make me look ugly, Deputy?" She batted her eyes.

"Not at all. I don't think anything could do that."

Mandy smiled and batted her eyes some more. Gary knew girls like Mandy needed to be complimented a lot and figured it was the best way to proceed with his line of questioning.

"Do you really think so?" she asked.

"Are you kidding? You're probably the prettiest girl in town. Everyone knows that. You must see the way all the guys look at you."

"You're embarrassing me, Deputy Forsyth."

"Well, I didn't mean to do that. I just meant you shouldn't worry about that bump on your head too much. It will go away in a couple days, and no one will ever notice."

She slid closer to him across the cruiser's large front seat. Gary took his eyes off the road for a moment and looked at her; she smiled back at him. His plan was backfiring. Now she thought he was trying to hit on her. *Quick, jackass, change the subject.*

"So, you've been dating this guy from the power company?" he asked.

The question didn't seem to faze Mandy all that much; she continued to smile at him as if he was a late-night snack. Gary's heart raced as his palms went slick against the wheel. He had steered the conversation in the wrong direction and struggled to get it back on track.

"Felix, you said his name was, right?"

"Yeah, Felix, Felix Castillo. He's a nice guy. We went to see *The Amityville Horror* last Saturday at the movies."

"That sounds nice. Did you go to the Warren Drive-in?"

She slid closer.

"Uh-huh." Mandy bit her lip as she answered. "The Warren Drive-in." Her voice had gone raspy, sounding as if she'd just woken up or she was deliberately trying to sound sexier.

Gary was glad the entrance to her apartment was just up on the right. He used the turn signal and pulled into the parking lot.

"You were talking to Felix before you fell by the dumpster?"

"I think we were in the alley," she answered, her voice dreamy and far away.

Forsyth began to feel a bit lightheaded himself. He blinked a few times as he guided the cruiser through the lot and pulled into a parking place.

"You and Felix were in the alley; what were you doing in the alley?" Gary's eyes felt heavy; it suddenly became difficult for him to keep them open. He tried to shake it but was unable. He felt like he had been drugged. *God, did she drug me?* He tried to remember if Mandy had been near his coffee. He thought it was possible. He tried to move his hands, but they were just too heavy.

Mandy slid her body up against him and whispered in his ear. "Well, we were in the alley so Felix could fuck me." She grabbed the deputy's crotch and began to rub him.

Gary couldn't move. A wave of heat washed over him like a shot of morphine. He tried to resist but couldn't; she must have drugged him. He waited for her to remove the pistol from his holster. *How could I have been so stupid?* He had completely underestimated this clever, clever girl.

Mandy pressed her mouth to his ear and slipped her tongue into it. He shivered from the chill that entered him. It felt as if she were penetrating his brain. Bright white light flashed in his eyes as her tongue buried deeper into his ear canal.

Then Mandy unbuttoned his pants and unzipped his fly. Forsyth couldn't tell if he was still breathing. Her hand burned like a cinder as she grabbed him. She took it out and stroked it violently. It was painful yet wonderful at the same time. He was helpless to stop her, not that he entirely wanted to. She leaned forward and put him into her mouth. Her head moved up and down as every muscle in the deputy's body seized. She continued the motion until he began to convulse. She brought him to the edge and then sent him over. Gary experienced the most powerful orgasm he had ever had in his life.

Gary stiffened in excruciating pain as something entered him. It slid into his guts and exploded; it had come from the girl's mouth. His eyes rolled back into his skull as the sensation ripped into him like a blade. Deputy Forsyth passed out as Mandy shared her gift with him, just as Felix had shared it with her.

The girl finished what she had been instructed to do. Then she checked her makeup in the mirror as the deputy sat behind the wheel convulsing with drool spilling from his bottom lip.

Mandy straightened her skirt and exited the cruiser. She let herself into the apartment and walked up the steps.

"Hello, Jackie," she called to her roommate. "I've got something I want to show you." The black onyx of her eyes reflected the hallway light as she made her way to the bedroom where Jackie lay sleeping.

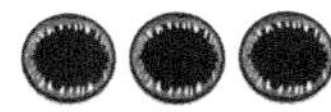

The top of Carl's head lined up perfectly with the hinge of the light above the autopsy shelf. Several strands of what appeared to be Felix Castillo's hair, along with a piece of his scalp, had been caught in the mechanism's retractable arm. Which made no sense. If someone had come into the morgue and removed the body, they certainly would have had to move the light. There was no other way. Burt and Carl remained silent for a moment longer, trying to register the implied impossibility. Carl's analytical mind reached for a tangible rationalization, while Burt's less grounded imagination was off to the races.

"I don't get it," Burt said, finally breaking the silence. "I just don't get it."

Carl swung his legs over the side and hopped off the shelf. Burt handed him his hat. "I've heard you say that sometimes during an autopsy, a cadaver can move on its own. Tell me about that."

A wash of relief softened Burt's face. "Of course. That has to be it. You know, I thought for a second there that old Felix here just kind of—" Burt held his arms and walked a few steps like Frankenstein's monster.

The sheriff held up his hands to stop his friend. "Could we please focus here, Burt? I'm starting to get a headache, and I got a lot on my plate right now."

"You're right. I'm sorry." The coroner lowered his arms. "Well, as a cadaver goes into a state of rigor mortis, the body does a whole bunch of crazy shit."

"Crazy shit, that's the clinical definition?" Carl asked.

"Cadaveric spasms, or postmortem spasms," Burt clarified. "The muscles and ligaments start to contract and tighten. The gasses in the body escape, and, well, it's pretty disgusting. Sometimes, an arm will twitch, and it could even shoot up into the air."

The sheriff nodded his head. "Could a body sit up from a prone position?" he asked.

"It's not impossible." Burt seemed pleased. "That must be what happened."

"That's what happened, huh? Well, during the rigor mortis process, is it common for a body to also climb off the damn table and let itself out the back door?"

"No." Burt knew it was no time to be clever. "Someone had to come in and remove the body."

"That doesn't make a whole lot of sense." Carl squinted. "Who the hell goes around stealing bodies from the morgue?"

Burt figured it was best not to say anything and shrugged his shoulders.

"You know, Burt, I'm gonna have to question your men and get their stories. I don't even know how I am supposed to report this. You have any idea how this will look when I tell the State Police there's been a murder and we seem to have lost the body?" Carl took a deep breath. "Do you have any idea how that looks, Burt?"

"It looks pretty bad."

"It looks terrible." Carl took his cowboy hat off and scratched his head. "On top of this, I got Dr. Malcolm about to quarantine the dang medical center."

"Hold on, what quarantine? You didn't say anything about a quarantine."

"It's not like you gave me a chance. I'm trying to conduct a murder investigation, and I get a call that my medical examiner has lost the body."

"All right," Burt said. "I deserve that. I do. So, what's this about quarantine? What's going on?"

"Well, it's possible I may have exposed you to a virus."

"What?!" Burt shouted. "A virus?"

"Dr. Malcolm isn't sure. He needs to run more tests before he knows anything. But last night, three kids were admitted into the emergency room with similar symptoms."

"What the hell's wrong with them?" Burt asked.

"Thought it was the flu, at first, started a couple days ago. High fever, chills, body aches and pains," Carl explained.

"That sounds like the flu to me."

"There's more. The Boyle kid stopped breathing for nearly three minutes. The doctors were able to bring him back, but he's on a ventilator now. Also, the Richards twins were having seizures, and the little girl started losing her teeth."

"Jesus Christ, Carl. It sounds like those kids have been poisoned." Burt sprinted out the door toward his office.

"Where the hell are you going?" Carl called to him.

"I've come across something like that before."

Carl followed Burt into the office; his friend had removed several books from the shelf next to his desk and began flipping through the pages.

"You really think it sounds like poisoning?" the sheriff asked.

Burt continued to rifle through the pages, not hearing his friend's question.

"You might be able to help out at the center. I'm sure Dr. Malcolm could use all hands on deck. It's not like you have an autopsy to perform at the moment."

"Is there any way the children could have come in contact with the same substance?" Burt asked.

Carl nodded. "I suppose; they don't live all that far apart ... Damn! The kids practically live next door to each other."

Burt looked up from the manual with concern on his face. "Where do they live?"

"Oh shit," Carl said under his breath. "The Richards twins live on Mountain Ave, and the Boyle kid lives on Foothills Drive. Their houses are only separated by a small stretch of woods."

"You're shitting me, right?"

The sheriff continued. "I'm not shitting you. We were right in front of the Boyle kid's house this morning. That's where the body was found."

CHAPTER 16

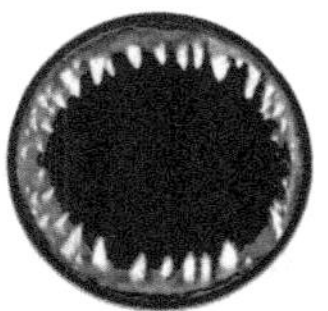

Before dinner, Troy gave his mother and father a tour of Scream in the Dark. Neither of them had seen the finished project. Lois had been around while the boys were building it but given them their privacy. Don had promised Troy he would assist with the construction, but when the cave was discovered and the shit had hit the fan, he had to go back on his word. He'd been put in charge of the whole cave fiasco, which meant long days and even some night shifts. He swore he would make it up to his son and said he would be there the night of the party. Which was another promise Donald Fischer was unable to keep.

Don's responsibilities at the quarry were already demanding without the added aggravation the recent find presented. He was the geological engineer for DuCain and one of only a handful of men in the state certified in demolitions. The weekly blasting that occurred on-site was executed under Don Fischer's direct guidance and supervision. It was the crux of the process that earned the men of DuCain their bread and butter. Now he had additional responsibilities to contend with. He was in charge of maintaining the integrity of the cavern until the proper authorities arrived tomorrow, and then he was supposed to act as some type of spokesperson-slash-liaison once they did. Don was to give them whatever they needed to make their work easier so they could get the hell off his job site as fast as possible. Which meant more time away from home.

The long hours were only part of what kept Don from his fatherly and husbandly duties. He'd been consumed with work long before the cavern was discovered. Even when he was home, he was never entirely there. Troy had noticed it a little, and Lois quite a bit more.

"You did this all by yourself?" Don asked as the three of them stepped into a room filled with spiders. Standing well over six feet tall, he needed to duck to avoid brushing against the glow-in-the-dark arachnids. Even in his thirties, Don had a baby face and been told more than a few times that he resembled a certain member of the Fab Four.

"Well, Rob helped too," Troy answered.

Don hadn't meant to remind him. "I'm impressed, kiddo."

"Sheriff Primrose thinks I could work in the movie business one day." Troy brightened a bit.

"The movie business." Don lifted his brow. "Is that something you're interested in?"

"I don't know, never thought about it before. Sounds kinda cool, though."

They walked over the rubber hoses on the floor and stepped into the graveyard room.

"Wow," Don exclaimed. "This is something else. I feel like I'm in a vampire movie."

Troy stepped over the small fence and walked up to the coffin lying on the floor.

"I brought them inside and then came over here to investigate. Eric was in the coffin. He grabbed me and pretended to bite my neck. Everyone got so scared, but they couldn't get out because Billy was holding the door shut. It was awesome!" Troy beamed with pride.

"You've got quite an imagination, kiddo," Don said. "You would be a great movie director or producer."

"Director ... producer, what do they do?" Troy looked at his mother.

"I'm not really sure, honey."

"Well, they're the guys in charge of everything. They're the ones who come up with all the ideas," Don told him.

"Oh," Troy looked as if he were concentrating intensely. "Sheriff Primrose said something about being a set designer."

"Sure," Don agreed. "Those are the guys who build the stuff. But I see you as a creator, a thinker. The producers are the real thinkers. You liked *Star Wars*, right? Well, George Lucas produced and directed it. Who do you think thought of R2D2?"

"Steven Spielberg too," Lois added. "He made *Jaws* and *Close Encounters of the Third Kind*."

"Then that's what I wanna be when I grow up. A producer or director like George Lucas and Steven Spielberg. I'll make a vampire movie, but not in black and white. Something super scary with a crazy haunted house in it." A massive grin spread across Troy's face as he explained.

"I'd pay to see that," Don said.

"So would I," Lois agreed. "Say, who's ready for dinner?"

"I am." Troy was always ready to eat and had been growing out of his clothes a little too quick for Lois's liking. She wished he could stay young for just a bit longer.

"Why don't you go get washed up, and your father and I will follow you in a second," she said.

Troy ran out of the garage and left Lois and Don in the graveyard. She folded her arms and looked at him.

"This is where I found them. It was horrible. Rob was having a seizure. I thought for sure he was going to die." She paused, then added: "You really should have been here."

Don shook his head and exhaled deeply. "You know I can't help it, Lois. Old man DuCain put me in charge of the whole site. This damn cave fiasco has my hands tied. They need me up there a little more these days."

"What about us? We need you too. Troy needed his father's help; this was so important to him."

"He did a pretty good job on his own. I'm sure Troy understands." Don raised his hands and shrugged. "He's fine."

"Don't be so sure about that. Rob nearly died last night, and he isn't out of the woods yet. Trust me, Don, Troy isn't fine."

"I didn't mean it like that," he tried to explain. "Believe me, I wish I could have been here. But things are crazy right now. What do you want from me?"

There it was. They were the exact words he used years ago back in college. Lois had been infuriated then and wanted to tear his eyes out. *"What do you want from me?"* he had asked her. The memory made her want to slap him still today.

Lois Middleton met Donald Fischer at Penn State during the spring of 1969. He had been working towards his master's, studying geosciences, and tutoring math to make a little extra cash. Lois was an English major working towards a degree in literature. When it came to prose and composition, she was a wiz, but she had taken statistics as one of her electives and was lost in the class. Her professor had recommended she either find a tutor or accept the statistical probability she might fail the course.

She saw a bulletin board in the student lounge with a list of tutors and took down a few numbers. Donald Fischer had agreed to help her with her math. The first thing she noticed about the boy was how much he looked like Paul McCartney, with his shaggy Beatles haircut and pretty boy complexion. She felt guilty for thinking he was cute since Carl was still her boyfriend, even though he was miles away in Garrett Grove.

They met three times a week to study statistics and probabilities. Donald was funny and made her laugh, and Lois had begun to receive passing grades, thanks to his tutelage.

The war in Vietnam was in full swing, and it was common to see organized rallies on campus. Also, there was a large population of kids being referred to as hippies. Lois and Don didn't exactly fit that category despite Don's long hair. But they did enjoy the music played at the bars on campus and some of the local bands.

He asked her out one Friday night; his friend's band was playing in Altoona. At first, she declined, but Don wouldn't take no for an answer.

"Just a friendly date," he said. "I swear, I'll be a perfect gentleman."

He was very charming, and Lois had to admit she really did want to go. So, she agreed to join him.

They made the drive to Altoona and enjoyed the show. The band played songs from Jefferson Airplane, Grateful Dead, and Jimi Hendrix. They drank Yuengling beer, which was brewed right there in Pennsy, and they had a great time.

Lois felt guilty being infatuated with the cute senior. But she couldn't help it. And somewhere between the beer and the music, she stopped thinking about Carl. She told herself it was because she'd been drunk; that's why she had slept with Don. At least that's what she told herself the first time. The second time she couldn't use that excuse. Then she said it was because she was lonely. After that, she stopped making excuses. By that point, she was just having fun.

She enjoyed her Friday nights with Don and had started to avoid Carl's calls. But Lois felt horrible and completely torn. She loved Carl; he had been her first, and they had planned a future together. But Don was intelligent, had dreamy eyes, and was a respected senior on campus; when she was with him, she felt respected too.

They had sat in the front seat of his car one night, smoking cigarettes and drinking Yuengling. "What are your plans after college?" she asked him.

"Well, after graduation, I think I'll take a couple months off to travel a little, you know, see the country a bit."

She rested her head on his shoulder and listened to his heartbeat. "I mean after that, what are your plans for the future?"

"Oh, that's easy. I'm applying to the Yosemite Geological Society in California to study the fault line and tectonic shift."

"I have no idea what you're talking about," she said and kissed him.

"I don't expect you to," he said. "It's just more boring geology stuff. Not very exciting at all, at least not to most people. Guess I'm a nerd."

"Maybe a little, but that's okay." She rubbed his chest hair. "What else? Do you see yourself getting married or having kids? I bet you'd make a good father."

"Na, not me," he said. "I need to focus on my career and get on my feet before getting married. I feel like I need to do things in the right order. First, make money, have the career and the house. At least, that's the plan."

"That makes sense," she said. It was then Lois realized their relationship had been nothing more than a college fling. Don hadn't been all that serious about her, and although she'd been infatuated with him, that was probably all there was to it. She enjoyed the time they'd spent together but suddenly felt guilty for dating him behind Carl's back. That's when she decided she would stop seeing Don.

Two weeks later, Lois found out she was pregnant. She cried for nearly a week straight before she built up the nerve to talk to Don about it. She didn't know how he would react; actually, she had a good idea and was regretting it. She didn't expect anything from him and was pretty sure that's how he would want it as well. Still, he was the father, and he deserved to know.

They met at the student center; it was where he first agreed to tutor her.

"Lois, how have you been?" he greeted her as he sat down.

She faked a smile and gave him a peck on the cheek. "I've been better, to tell you the truth."

"What's wrong?" He looked concerned and took her hand.

Lois sat there trying to find the words and braced herself for his reaction. She had cried so much over the past week and could feel she was about to start again. She held it in for as long as she could, then burst into tears.

"What's wrong, honey? Tell me." His voice almost comforting.

"I'm sorry, don't hate me," she said. "I—I'm pregnant, Don." She hadn't felt any better.

He sat there with his mouth open as if he were waiting for a fly to come along and land on his tongue. His face had gone white as he stared at her.

"Please say something."

"Um, you're sure?" he asked awkwardly.

"I'm sure."

"It's mine?" Lois glared at him. "I mean, of course it's mine, I just ... well. How did this happen?"

She gave him the same look. "I think you remember how it happened. You were there."

"I-I know how it happened, but I thought we were careful. We made sure, you know."

"These things aren't a hundred percent. There's always a chance. I guess this is one of those times." She watched him fidgeting in his chair. *This is horrible.*

"So, what's next?" He looked at her as if she should have it all figured out by now.

Lois hated him for that. She didn't expect anything from him. She just thought the right thing to do was tell him she was going to have his baby. She immediately regretted the decision. "I don't know what's next," she snapped. "I go back to Garrett Grove, and I raise my baby. That's what you usually do with them." She continued to cry.

"What about ... um, you know," he said under his breath.

"An abortion?!" she shouted, attracting the attention of over half the students in the center.

Donald's face turned beet red, and he motioned for her to keep it down.

Lois lowered her voice. "I'm not getting an abortion from some backstreet butcher. I would never. I am going back home, and I am going to have my baby. I just thought I should tell you, that's all."

"What do you want from me?" he asked, and she had hated him even more. *How dare you put that on me, you bastard!*

"I don't want anything from you, Donald," she hissed, then stood up and walked out the door.

"Lois, wait." He ran after her. "Wait!" He caught up and stopped her. "That came out all wrong; you caught me off guard, that's all." Lois turned on him, ready to strike. "Look, I'm not going to let you run off, and I'm not going to leave this all on your shoulders. This isn't just your responsibility."

"Stop, Don. You don't want this." She offered him the out; all he had to do was walk away.

"Don't tell me what I want, Lois. I can't let you do this on your own. That's my baby too." Donald took her hand and pulled her close.

"Don't do this." She allowed him to comfort her. And then she allowed him to make an even bigger mistake.

Lois agreed to marry Donald Fischer even though she knew he didn't love her and doubted she had ever loved him. It seemed like the right thing to do for the baby. She would finish the semester and then return to Garrett Grove. Donald would stay and finish out the year and graduate with his degree. Then they would get married and find a house somewhere close to her parents. It wasn't the way she had planned for her life to end up, but it was still a plan. It had all been so difficult up until that point, but the hardest thing she would ever have to do was still ahead of her; she had to tell Carl. She owed him the truth.

She called him and had been straight with him, for the most part. She told him about the baby and about Donald in not so many words. But Carl had asked her questions she simply couldn't answer. He asked if she loved Donald, and she had remained silent. She couldn't say yes; it would have been a lie. But she couldn't tell him no either. She knew Carl would have tried to talk her into coming home and letting him support both her and the baby. And she couldn't let him do that. She had already hurt him enough. In the end, she never said a word, and allowed Carl to think what he would. She wasn't sure if it was the cruelest thing she'd ever done or the kindest.

Lois made the trip home the same weekend a certain young priest was making his way down the New York State Thruway. Neither of them ended up where they thought they would. Lois Middleton Fischer and Father Kieran McCabe had discovered the same thing in very different ways, that no matter what your plans might be for the future, God's plans would always come as a surprise. There was nothing a little girl from Garrett Grove or a priest from Utica could do to change that.

Don graduated with his master's degree, moved to Garrett Grove, and married Lois. He got a job as a geological engineer for DuCain Industries and never made it to Yosemite. Troy was born later that year and quickly became the apple of his mother's eye. He had been a breech baby and nearly killed Lois on the way out. She'd been unable to have any more children afterward, which may have had a little to do with the incredible bond between the two of them. Troy had her blue eyes and sensitive heart, and he inherited Donald's intellect, which was a good thing, but other than that, he was a momma's boy.

Don loved Troy just as much as his wife did, but he wasn't the most affectionate of fathers. It just wasn't how he'd been raised. And since Don spent his days at work while Lois stayed home with Troy, it was only natural the boy would have a stronger bond with his mother.

Now, standing amidst the cardboard graveyard of Scream in the Dark, Lois stared at Don with her arms folded and her face turning redder by the second. "What do I want from you?" she repeated. "I want you to act like you give a shit about your son and spend some time with him. That's what I want from you."

"I am doing everything I can to keep a roof over our heads and food on the table." Don counted his sacrifices using his fingers to accentuate his point. "I go to work every day so you can be here when Troy comes home from school. I can't help that it keeps me from being around the house. I got responsibilities." His voice rose to a shout.

"Rob could die. Do you have any idea what our son is going through right now?" Lois threw her arms up in the air. "I guarantee, Troy is not fine. He might act like he is okay, but he doesn't know what to think. Rob is his best friend, has been since his first day of kindergarten. Could you at least act like you care?"

Don took a defensive step backward and attempted to make peace. "I don't want to fight here. I'll talk to him, all right?"

But Lois wasn't hearing it. It was always the same story. "Just talk to your son and spare me the bullshit!" she shouted.

Troy heard his parents from where he stood outside the garage. They were fighting about him again; it seemed like every time they fought, his name was brought up. He knew it was his fault that they were having such a hard time getting along but had no idea what he had done. *Maybe it's my grades. I swear I'll clean my room when you ask. Please stop fighting.* A hundred different reasons presented themselves; not one of them even came close to identifying the root cause of his parents' problems. Troy wiped the wetness from his cheeks and listened as they continued to yell at one other.

"Rob is his best friend, has been since the first day of kindergarten." The voice of his mother carried to where he stood in the driveway.

No!

He knew Rob was sick, but not for a minute had he thought his friend could actually die. The tears came faster and harder. *Rob can't die.* They had known each other for as long as Troy could remember; he was his best friend, his only friend, and had been since ...

Troy remembered that very first day of kindergarten. It was so long ago, and he had been so little. It was hard to recall all the details. The conversation about school was something his mother had kept bringing up, and he remembered feeling excited about the idea of it, at first. Then the day finally arrived and all the fear along with it. He had never been away from his parents without at least the comfort of his grandparents to fill the void. The idea of it suddenly became a very scary reality.

Lois had dressed him in what she called his school clothes and fussed over his hair till she finally said it was perfect. She let him sit in the front seat of the car like a grownup, which made him feel important. Then they pulled up to a big yellow building that Troy had never seen before, and panic started to set in. She held his hand as they walked through the front doors into an enormous hallway; the ceiling was so high it made Troy feel tiny, like an insect on the sidewalk. The place smelled funny too, like the stuff his mom used to clean the bathroom, which made him even more uneasy.

There were other people there as well, looking at him, watching what he and his mother were doing. A woman and a little girl walked ahead of them, then disappeared behind a large door. A moment later, the woman exited alone, holding a tissue to her eyes, trying to hide the fact that she was crying.

His mom had looked down at him, smiled, and squeezed his hand, but it didn't give him the confidence it was intended to.

He recalled the door opening onto what appeared to be an army of people. There were long tables set with small chairs lining either side. Little boys and girls packed into the room accompanied by their mothers, and everyone was talking at once.

"You must be Troy," a pretty woman said to him.

He nodded yes but was too overwhelmed to speak.

She bent down closer to eye level. "I'm Miss Boriello, and I am going to be your kindergarten teacher. It's very nice to meet you, Troy." She had long brown hair and wore a kind smile, and Troy liked her already, which put him somewhat at ease, but he was far from comfortable.

Miss Boriello and his mother exchanged a few words, and his mom nodded. Then she led Troy to an empty seat next to where a young Robert Boyle sat talking to his mother.

"Hi, my name's Rob. What's yours?" the little boy asked.

"T ... Troy," he replied.

"Don't be scared, Troy," Rob said. The boy seemed awfully grown up, and Troy liked that. "My mom said we're going to get cookies and juice later."

Troy wondered why his mother hadn't told him about the cookies. That was probably why everyone in the room was so excited. Overstimulation made his head spin; the scene was a cross between a parade and a circus, with children talking over one another and mothers struggling to be heard above the commotion.

That was when Miss Boriello walked to the front of the room and spoke. "Mothers, it's time." And the moms reacted as if it had been rehearsed. Lois bent down and wiped her cheeks.

"I love you, honey. Have a great first day of school. I'll be back in a couple hours." She kissed him and slowly walked to the door along with all the other mothers.

What's happening? Alarms went off in his head. *What?* She was leaving him here with all these strangers? She couldn't do that. "Mommy, no!" he cried as she walked out the door wiping her eyes.

The last of the mothers left, and the place erupted like a volcano. Children jumped up and chased after them. They pounded on the giant door as Troy sat in his seat, frightened and confused. Most of the kids began to scream and cry, but he was still unable to move. He looked to his right and noticed the boy named Rob had remained in his chair as well. The vivid memory became a snapshot image seared in his mind. It would never leave and was probably the cornerstone of what would make Troy Fischer and Robert Boyle inseparable best friends.

Miss Boriello stood silent at the front of the room and allowed the pandemonium to ensue for several moments. Then, she began to rummage through a brown grocery bag sitting on her desk.

Troy couldn't remember if he had cried but was pretty sure he had. He was overwhelmed by the panic going on around him but was comforted by how Rob handled it. That was probably the only reason Troy didn't freak out.

Rob sat with his hands folded, a perfectly behaved little boy, while the other kids in the room went ballistic. He appeared unfazed by the insanity that threatened to rip Troy from his chair at any moment. Then, something happened that Troy would never forget. A single tear rolled down Rob's cheek and clung to his chin for a moment. It wasn't followed by a second or a third, and Rob made no attempt to wipe it away. Even to Troy's five-year-old perception, the moment struck him as significant. And from that day on, Troy Fischer and Robert Boyle were as thick as thieves; neither hell nor high water could keep them apart.

Miss Boriello had set up paper plates and called out over the cacophony, "Who wants chocolate chip cookies?"

The screaming ebbed to a dull roar. The children had something else to focus on. And that was Troy's memory of his first day of school. Chocolate chip cookies, Rob Boyle, and a single tear. It was a memory that would last him the rest of his life.

CHAPTER 17

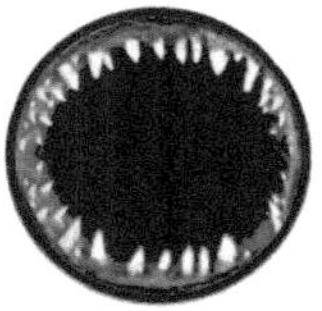

Ethan Ziegler sat in his office staring at the toxicology results. All three cases yielded identical conclusions: bloodborne pathogen. The children had ingested the same contaminant, a poison that infected the blood. However, this poison was unlike any he had seen before. It possessed the qualities of a parasitic bacterium, along with some other anomalous attributes as well.

The only good news: it wasn't an airborne contagion. The contaminant had to enter the body through either an exchange of fluids, transfusion, or ingestion. As far as he could tell from the blood work and the lab results, there was no need to worry about an outbreak. Which didn't make him feel much better. He still had no idea what the children had gotten into and no clue how to help them. Antibiotics were doing little if anything to fight the bacteria. But their fevers had gone down somewhat, and none of the patients had experienced any more seizures throughout the day, which was a good sign. Perhaps they simply had to let their own metabolism do the job. That was if their immune systems didn't kill them first. At the rate their white blood cells were attacking the red, it was amazing they were alive at all. Ziegler still had no answer as to how their organs had mutated at such a rapid rate. And although the threat of quarantine was over, the children's struggle to survive had just begun.

Dr. Malcolm woke precisely two hours after he had fallen asleep. He showered, had a cup of coffee, and was back at Chilton before the sun set. He passed through the emergency room, greeted his staff, and checked on the new arrivals. There had been only one; Denny Birch arrived with a Hula Popper fishing lure firmly attached to the side of his head. The man had spent Sunday afternoon fishing the banks of the Lenape River under the Gables Bridge when he hooked a decent-sized brook trout. He attempted to set the hook and jerked the line a bit too hard, yanking the lure completely out of the fish's mouth. The Hula Popper rocketed like a guided missile, out of the water and right back at him. Four out of six hooks now pierced the man's cheek and forehead. Denny claimed he wasn't in any pain. The Jack Daniels he'd been drinking since eleven a.m. may have had something to do with that. It also might have played a part in his momentary loss of muscular coordination as well.

Dr. Freedman, a gangly man with coke-bottle glasses, was busy removing the lure when Malcolm passed through the ER. He stopped and looked while Freedman snipped one of the hooks with a set of pliers. "Catch anything today, Denny?" Malcolm asked.

"A couple. You should have seen the one that did this to me, had to be close to five pounds, Doc," the man slurred.

"Ahh, the one that got away. Well, there's always next week." Dr. Malcolm continued his rounds. "Carry on, gentlemen."

The place was quiet, which was typical for a Sunday evening. Dr. Malcolm nodded to the nurse at the front desk, who was relatively new and filled in for Nurse Gilmartin on her nights off. He entered the hallway and headed directly towards Dr. Ziegler's office. A young candy striper turned the corner as he passed the lab. The sound of the girl's shoes squeaking on the freshly buffed floor echoed off the walls. He finally arrived at his destination and walked into the office. The young doctor sat at a desk with several reports in front of him.

"Dr. Malcolm, I'm glad you're here." Ziegler stood up and shook the chief's hand.

"So, what have we got, son?" Dr. Malcolm asked. He took a seat in front of the desk, and Dr. Ziegler returned to his own.

"Well, take a look at this, sir." He handed a clipboard to the old doctor. "I've run the blood and toxicology, and I think we've narrowed it down a bit."

Dr. Malcolm removed a pair of bifocals from his coat pocket and looked at the front page of the clipboard. He studied it for a long moment in silence. Then he flipped to the next page and examined that as well. "Any idea what type of toxin they ingested?" he asked.

"That's where things get a bit strange, I'm afraid." Dr. Ziegler handed him another report. Malcolm studied it.

"Parasite?" He turned back to the blood work. "I don't feel very relieved. I'm glad to hear it isn't a virus, but this is rather inconclusive. A bacterial parasite doesn't mean the community is safe from infection. Granted, they would have to come in contact with the same substance or source as the children. Which means we need to figure out where these kids have been in the past week."

Dr. Ziegler rubbed his eyes. He'd been on the floor for over twenty-four hours and only gotten a few minutes sleep here and there. "I've been working on that and was about to go talk to the parents. But I wanted to have some answers before I did, and I wanted to talk to you first. I thought about asking Burt Lively to check out the school tomorrow, and then get permission to check out the kids' bedrooms. They could have picked up something in the classroom or on the playground."

"If that were the case, I think we would have a lot more than three sick kids. But it couldn't hurt." He looked at his young protégée. "You look like hell. When was the last time you slept, Doctor?"

Ziegler leaned back in his chair and attempted to stifle a yawn. "I had a few winks here and there, but I've been on the floor for over twenty-four hours now."

"I appreciate your dedication, Dr. Ziegler, but I think you better go home for the night. I'm sorry I left so much on your plate; I couldn't have trusted anyone else to get the job done. I knew I could count on you."

Ziegler did a double take. "Thank you, Doctor. But we're still far from knowing what's going on here. I could stay a bit longer and help out."

"Absolutely not! You're no good to anybody half asleep. Now go home and get some rest. That's an order. Dr. Freedman and the rest of the staff are here. I'll check in on the kids and talk to the parents. Then I'll call Burt first thing in the morning and see what his schedule looks like." Dr. Malcolm stood up and opened the door.

"Are you sure, sir?" Ziegler asked.

"Absolutely; see you tomorrow, son." He exited and turned down the hall toward the ICU.

Carl steered the cruiser north toward the Richards house on Mountain Ave with Burt sitting next to him in the passenger seat. The body of

Felix Castillo had disappeared from the medical examiner's office in broad daylight, and there was no explanation other than the possibility it had been stolen. It was a slim possibility at that, but Carl didn't rule it out since it was almost Halloween. He'd seen teenagers do some pretty stupid things this time of year, although nothing quite as bizarre as messing with the dead. At the moment, it was the only working theory.

Carl picked up the radio handset and spoke. "Sheriff Primrose to base. Come in, Tara." He let go of the button.

"This is Andrea, Sheriff. Tara went home an hour ago. I've been trying to reach you for a while. I guess you were away from your radio." Andrea Geary was the night dispatcher and relieved Tara Jefferies at five o'clock on Sundays. *Jeez, is it that late already?* He had been running around like a one-legged man in an ass-kicking contest all day and barely had time to eat the sandwich Burt shared with him at the lab.

"I didn't realize it was so late. What's up, Andrea?"

"We've had two separate calls in the last hour. One from Sarah Negal and the other from Beth Campbell. Their sons went out earlier today on their bicycles and were supposed to be home hours ago."

"Well, it's not like the kids even missed dinner yet. I wouldn't be surprised if they lost track of time and are out playing somewhere. They'll find their way home as soon as they get hungry."

"I suppose you're right, Sheriff. I said the same thing." Andrea's voice broke up. "I told them I would contact you and let you know about the missing boys."

"They're not missing, Andrea," he corrected her. "It hasn't even been a full afternoon yet. Trust me, boys have a way of losing track of time, especially at that age. What grade are they in?"

"I believe Jeff and Tommy are in the fourth grade." Burt looked at Carl. The Richards kids and Robert Boyle were in the fourth grade as well.

"Well, like I said, I'm sure the boys will be walking through their front doors any minute. Who's on duty tonight?"

"That's the other reason I was trying to get a hold of you, Sheriff," Andrea said, her voice breaking up again. She had a habit of putting her mouth too close to the microphone. Every time she did, her voice cracked and distorted. At least she didn't say "over" after every sentence like Tara did. She continued. "Deputy Rainey and Deputy Kovach are on tonight, but that's not why I was calling. Deputy Forsyth was en route to the Con Ed plant in Warren to check out a lead on the Castillo case."

The Sheriff waited for her to continue. *Maybe it would be better if she did say over.* "Is there anything else, Andrea?"

"I haven't been able to get in contact with him for a few hours now. He doesn't answer his radio, and I even tried him at home. No luck there either."

"Did you try reaching him at the power plant?" He figured the answer was yes but still had to ask.

"That's the thing, Sheriff. He never showed up at the plant. He told one of the supervisors he was on his way. But I called up there an hour ago, and he never made it." The static stopped when she released the button on the mic.

Carl looked at Burt; neither man said a word. He wondered if he'd gotten the dates mixed up and it was April Fool's and not the week before Halloween. Burt looked out the passenger window and pretended not to listen.

"I'm sure Gary will show up at the station or the plant any minute now. Keep trying to reach him. I'm with Burt Lively, and we're on our way to the Richards residence on Mountain Ave to check out a lead."

"A lead? On the Castillo case, Sheriff?" she asked.

He thought about the coincidence of the murder victim being found outside the home of Robert Boyle and the strange illness that had afflicted the children. "I'm not sure yet, Andrea. I'll let you know if I find something," he paused, "over," then replaced the handset.

The sun was low in the west, and the sky had just begun to turn purple. It would be dark soon, which would make it next to impossible to find anything.

Carl looked across the cab of the cruiser at his friend sitting in the passenger seat. "I'm not sure what we're looking for here, Burt. Do you think we're just going to stumble across whatever made those kids sick?"

"I don't know. But I'll bet all three of them play in those woods. I've always found in forensics to look for commonalities. If you ask me, the foothills that separated the Boyle and Richards houses are a pretty big commonality."

Carl smiled at his friend. "You wait till now to start making sense." He pulled the cruiser over to the side and parked near the Richards' driveway. He decided to enter the woods from the Mountain Ave side rather than Foothills Drive, due to what had taken place earlier that morning. He didn't want to raise any eyebrows and wanted to avoid answering any unnecessary questions from the neighbors. They exited the cruiser and cut through the yard, then took one of the paths into the foothills.

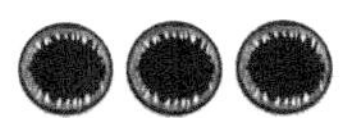

Dr. Ethan Ziegler felt guilty about leaving the center but was grateful Dr. Malcolm let him go; he was exhausted and had nearly fallen asleep at the wheel on his way home. But despite how tired he was, he had every intention of taking a quick shower and calling Jackie Gilmartin as soon as he freshened up.

The hot water hit him like a deep tissue massage, peeling away the past twenty-four hours like the skin of an onion. He sat on his bed in his bathrobe with plans of seeing the young nurse. But Ethan Ziegler never made it to the phone. He stretched out on the bed and was asleep before his head hit the pillow.

As Ethan Ziegler was closing his eyes, Erin Richards was opening hers. What had once been a normal ten-year-old girl barely looked human at all. Most of Erin's hair had fallen out; her long blonde locks lay beside her head on the pillow. Her skin hung loose on her face in flaps that resembled gills, sagging beneath her eyes and cheeks and the sides of her neck. It had lost its elasticity and no longer fit the child's face.

The eyes that stared up at the ceiling were as black as obsidian, with a secondary set of lids that blocked out much of the UV light from the overhead fluorescents.

The girl's lips had pulled back and grown thin, and her jaw had dislocated and dropped, allowing her mouth to hang open in an oval. It had only been an hour since the nurse checked on her, but most of the changes had occurred within the past fifteen minutes. Erin was mutating into something, and the process wasn't quite finished yet.

Sharp teeth erupted from her mouth like tiny arrowheads. A thick, black fluid coated them at the gum line as if she had begun to bleed oil.

The presence scanned the room, assessing every detail, taking in its surroundings. With every soul it devoured, it gained more knowledge. It consumed the essence of Erin Richards and assimilated her consciousness. Everything she had ever been was as much a part of it as the shaman of the creatures who had called themselves Lenape. All the beings it had consumed throughout the course of its lifespan were absorbed with one sole focus: evolution. Every thought and every memory of their fleeting existence added to its potency. It fed, it controlled them, and then it assimilated.

The creatures of the past had referred to it by many names. It had been called Nue and Vetala. Names like Penanggalan, Almesty, Ah Puch, and Ahk-Mah had been used, and more recently, the ones called Lenape had referred to it as Mantantu. It searched the minds of its new acquisitions; did they have a name? The one called Tommy had been thinking of one before it was consumed. The Jeff-creature had been thinking the same. They thought of the name as it ravaged them; they had called it ... Ojanox.

Every race had given it a name when their own existence was near an end. This civilization would call it Ojanox. It was pleased with this identity.

It searched the thoughts of Erin Richards and instructed her. The strange creature sat up and pulled the IV needle out of its arm. It studied the machines that monitored the child's vitals and focused its power at them. The heart monitor stopped working, and the other devices turned off as well. The Erin-creature threw her bare feet over the side of the bed. She had work to do.

CHAPTER 18

The sky had just begun to darken as Carl and Burt entered the woods behind the Richards house. They followed one of the dirt paths that had been cut into the foliage centuries ago by the Lenni Lenape Indians. The entire state had been home to the Lenape tribe, who believed Garrett Mountain possessed a divine connection to the spirit world. Burial sites were constantly being discovered in the Grove, and the kids in town were always turning up arrowheads.

Carl Primrose grew up in Garrett Grove and had scoured these very woods as a child. He played Davey Crockett and pretended he was Roy Rogers on the same path he and Burt now walked on.

The sun sank lower in the western sky, and long shadows stretched out before them. Carl removed a flashlight from his belt and focused the beam on either side of the path.

"What do you suppose we're looking for, Burt?'" Carl turned to his old friend, who was only inches behind him. "Jeez, give me a little room, would ya."

"You got the only flashlight, and I don't want to fall and twist an ankle. I'm having a hard enough time keeping up with those long legs of yours." Burt stayed right behind the sheriff.

"Well, try not to trip me in the process," Carl told him. "Any idea what we're looking for?" he asked again.

"No, not really," Burt replied. "But I got an idea we'll know it if we find it."

"That doesn't help much. What do you think, like mushrooms or a poison frog, or something like that?" Carl pointed the light onto the path in front of them. Daylight was fading fast; soon, it would be full dark and impossible to find anything.

"Hold on a second." Carl bent down and directed the light onto the soft ground in front of him. He studied the dirt, then checked the woods on either side of the trail.

"What do you see, Carl?" Burt asked.

"Probably nothing," he answered. "Couple sets of bicycle tires, pretty fresh by the looks of them too."

"Those kids your dispatcher told you about, they were out on their bikes when they went missing, weren't they?"

"They were." Carl studied the two distinct sets of tracks. One of the bikes had a thin tread that was worn out more on the left side than the right, and the other set had knobby treads. Carl thought they were possibly made by a three-speed and one of those small motocross bikes. He got up and started to follow them. "Try not to step directly on the tracks. Put your feet where I do." Carl showed him by walking on the side of the trail, not completely in the woods and not on the dirt.

"Okay," Burt told him. "Just go slow. It's getting dark as hell out here."

The tracks followed the path, and it became clear to Carl that the motocross bike had been trailing the three-speed, by the way the knobby treads overlapped the thinner ones. He also believed the marks had been made some time today. If they had been older, there would have been animal prints on top of them. There was a hell of a lot of critters in these woods.

"I can't see shit, Carl. We should come back in the morning." Burt tugged at the sheriff's arm.

Carl ignored him. Instead, he bent down and focused the light onto the dirt again. A large bootprint revealed itself in the soil. The grass and weeds on the right side of the path had been trampled; someone had cut through. The owner of the print had taken a few steps along the trail and then disappeared into the woods on the opposite side. The grass was disturbed in that direction as well. Then Carl measured the mark by placing his foot next to it and noticed the print was a good three sizes larger than his own size eleven. The guy who had left it was one big son of a bitch.

"I don't like this," Burt whined.

"Easy, old man. I'm not thrilled about it either, but I think we're on to something. Don't worry, I won't let anything happen to you."

A loud noise cut through the night; it came from the tree line on the side of the trail. The men stopped in their tracks as something large thrashed through the grass and fallen leaves. Something big stepped out of the woods in front of them and grunted. Carl jumped back, and Burt screamed.

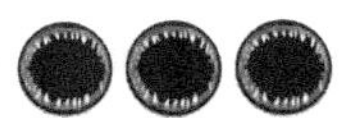

Dr. Malcolm passed the young candy striper on his way to the ICU. He nodded, and she returned the smile. The girl's name tag said Cyndi, not Cindy with a y at the end, but Cyndi with an i. "She looks like a Cyndi with an I," Malcolm muttered under his breath. The girl was young and blonde, somewhere around eighteen to twenty years old. He wondered if she had a crush on Dr. Ziegler. Now that was a contagion most of the young ladies at Chilton had contracted.

Before entering the ICU, Malcolm stopped in the changing room. He donned a protective paper gown, face mask, and eyewear. He also grabbed a fresh pair of surgical gloves. Now that they knew they were dealing with a parasitic bacterium, he didn't want to take any chances, since the method of transfer was still unknown. The protective garb reminded him of his time as the head of surgery back when Rosie was still alive. It had been a happy time for them. They'd been younger, and Rosie had still been relatively healthy; at least she hadn't been extremely unhealthy. His hair had been dark and thick, and Rosie, who had always been a full-size woman, was still a bit curvy. For some reason, John had done a lot more reflecting today than expected. He took a long, deep breath, hoping to catch a scent he knew he wouldn't find, and left the changing area.

The intensive care unit consisted of six individual rooms, occupying an independent wing of the medical center. Here, all the critical cases were referred as well as any patients who required solitary confinement. Since the Boyle child was the first to be admitted, Dr. Malcolm walked down the hall and opened the door to check on him first.

The room was bathed in a brilliant white light, so intense Malcolm's eyes were unable to adjust. Without warning, a sharp pain centered in the middle of his forehead. He grabbed his temples and nearly collapsed. Then his ears started to ring—loud and intense, like a whistle being blown inside his head. He rocked back and forth, swaying to a melody that only he could hear.

For a brief moment, John possessed the clarity to realize something was wrong, that he was in mortal danger. But the thought was silenced as if a blanket had been thrown over it. The ringing in his ears faded and was replaced by words he couldn't quite understand. And then he smelled it.

Faint, like the first flowers of spring, their fragrance caught on the breeze and carried through an open window. It lifted from the room and caressed his senses, gently but growing stronger by the second. *Estee ... Rosie's perfume.* But it was impossible; he had used the last of the bottle over a year ago. Still, it was as real as the memories that flooded his head and the voice that spoke to him. He heard it clearer now and could almost make out the words.

"Come sit with me, John," the voice said. "It's been so long since you sat with me."

John Malcolm knew that voice. How long had it been since the last time he heard it?

But John was so tired and found it almost impossible to keep his eyes open. He had no idea they were already closed.

The voice spoke again. "John, come sit with me."

It can't be; I have to be dreaming. John Malcolm forced himself to open his eyes and focused on the figure sitting on the bed in front of him.

The room wavered like a mirage, and the image faded into view. She sat before him, smiled, and patted the bed beside her. "Come sit with me, John."

He continued to sway in place as the vision grew clearer. "Rosie, what are you doing here?" he asked, an uneven smile infecting his face.

Rosie Malcolm sat on the bed, wearing a dress John had bought her over twenty years ago. He couldn't remember the last time he had seen it on her, but it had always been his favorite.

Her hair was exactly the way she had worn it back when he was the head of surgery. She would set it in curlers for hours just to get it right; John remembered she called it a bouffant. He thought it had made her look like Annette Funicello. Rosie looked good, exactly like she did in his dreams.

"What a silly question. I'm here to see you, of course," she said. "Now come over here and sit next to me, handsome."

John was propelled across the room, no longer in control of his own body. His arms hung limp at his sides, the clipboard fell from his grip and landed on the floor, the papers it held scattered. But John didn't notice. He stared into Rosie's deep, dark eyes. They were so dark they were almost black. *Rosie had green eyes*—the thought was silenced. He was drawn toward her as if a rope were fastened around his chest. There was no sense in resisting, not that he could if he wanted to. John's mind and body were no longer his own.

"Rosie," he said. A thin line of saliva fell from the side of his open mouth. "My Rosie."

His feet slid against the floor.

Rosie's smile grew wider. Her big, dark eyes focused intently on John as he approached the bed. Somehow, they grew darker and wider.

A strange thought echoed from somewhere within, something John had seen once in a cartoon. *Hey, Rosie, what big eyes you got ... to have.* A noise escaped from deep in his throat. It was intended to be a laugh but was closer to a whimper.

Rosie's smile broadened as if she knew what he was thinking and found it funny herself. Then, she opened her mouth and smiled, exposing at least three rows of razor-sharp teeth the size of broken Chiclets.

Hey, Rosie, what sharp teeth you got ... to have.

Carl and Burt collided, nearly sending each other sprawling into the woods as the beast emerged from the shadows and onto the path in front of them. Carl instinctively dropped his hand to the gun on his hip. With his other hand, he raised the flashlight in the direction of the creature. It grunted and then squealed as the light fell upon it. A large black sow had burst out of the darkness and stood in the middle of the path. It snorted a warning, then several piglets filed out of the woods. The little ones gathered around their momma, who stared down the path in the men's direction. They remained still while the sow sized them up. Once she was satisfied there was no threat and all her babies were accounted for, she darted into the woods on the opposite side of the trail, with her piglets close behind.

Carl, who had been holding his breath, released it. Wild pigs could be nasty and were known to attack, especially when it came to protecting their young. *That was too damn close.*

"I think I pissed myself," Burt said, sounding relieved.

Carl looked back at him and smiled. "Your secret's safe with me." He let out another deep breath and chuckled. "Because I think I might have pissed a little myself."

They laughed, thankful for the tension to have dissipated. Burt slapped Carl on his back. "Let's get out of here. We're not doing any good stumbling around in the dark."

"Yeah, I'm with you there." The sheriff directed the light across the path where the sow had stood with her babies. A glint of reflection flashed back at him from further down the trail; the beam bounced off something shiny and metallic.

"What the hell is that?" Burt asked.

But Carl was already walking toward the object.

The night grew silent and closed in around them. "Do you hear that?" Burt held his breath.

"Hear what? I don't hear anything," Carl replied.

"Exactly. What happened to all the crickets? They should be hollering up a storm." Burt followed Carl as the path took a gentle turn to the right. Finally, the light came to rest on the object that had caused the reflection.

Two bicycles lay overturned on the side of the trail. Carl approached and examined the tires. He motioned for Burt to be careful not to step on any of the tracks. One of the bikes had a thin tread and was in fact a three-speed. The other one had the name *Mongoose* written on the frame; it was a motocross bike with knobby treads. The bicycles lay half on the path and half off. Judging by the zigzag and skid marks, it looked to Carl as if the bikes had crashed into each other.

"I bet these belong to your two missing boys," Burt said.

"I'd have to agree. It looks like they were discarded in a hurry." The sheriff cast the light in the direction the bicycles had been heading. Then he lit up the woods on either side of the trail. "That's strange," he said, confused.

"This whole damn day has been strange," Burt said, looking over his shoulder into the darkness. "What part are you talking about?"

Carl cast the light on the area where the bikes lay. "Well, usually when you get off a bike, you step on the ground, but I don't see any footprints anywhere. It doesn't look like anyone even walked through the woods on either side."

The coroner followed the light to see what his friend was talking about and, sure enough, couldn't find any footprints near the bikes or on the trail. "That is strange," he said. "What do you make of it?"

"I haven't got a clue." Carl pulled his walkie-talkie from his hip. "Sheriff Primrose to base, come in, base."

Andrea's voice broke the silence with a garble of static. "Go ahead, Sheriff."

"I think I might have a lead on our two boys. You said they were out riding their bikes this morning?"

"It was a false alarm, Sheriff. Both of their mothers called; the kids came home for dinner just like you said."

Carl looked at Burt and shrugged. "They didn't happen to mention leaving their bikes out in the foothills, did they?"

"Neither of them mentioned anything. Why do you ask, Sheriff?"

"Well, I found two bicycles out here in the woods. Think it's odd someone would just leave them here."

"I can call back and check."

Carl pointed the light down the path and then back onto the trail. "Yeah, could you look into that for me? Has Deputy Forsyth checked in yet?"

"Still no word, Sheriff. He never made it to Con Ed either." Her voice broke up from being too close to the mic.

"Damn," he said under his breath. "Well, we're gonna head out and have another go at it in the morning. Have you heard anything from Dr. Malcolm?"

"Negative, Sheriff. Were you expecting him?"

"Probably not yet," he said. "Let me know what you find out about the bikes."

"Will do, Sheriff." Andrea terminated the transmission.

Burt Lively crept close enough to Carl that he was practically standing on top of him. He listened intently to the conversation and was more than ready to leave. "I got a bottle of scotch back at the lab. Thirsty?" he asked.

"If you're buying, I'm thirsty. Let's get the hell out of these damn woods, Burt," Carl replied.

It was the best thing Burt had heard all night.

The thing sitting on the bed next to Dr. John Malcolm looked nothing like his dead wife. It bore no resemblance to Robert Boyle, the child who had worn the skin that now covered the grotesquely mutated creature. And the stench that suffocated the room smelled nothing like Estee Lauder. It parted its lips, exposing the saw blade that had erupted from its gums. An oil-like saliva slipped out the side of its mouth as it manipulated the old doctor. Insatiable hunger radiated inside the small beast; euphoric intoxication consumed it as it prepared to strike. John Malcolm's eyes rolled back in his skull as the creature rushed forward. The presence poured into him and began to devour, gorging itself on consciousness and lifeblood. It nibbled away at the useful parts like a rat tearing through the trash. Munch ... munch ... munch!

CHAPTER 19

Dennis Richards sat in the cafeteria drinking a Tab and growing more impatient by the minute. Both of his kids were in the intensive care unit, and he wasn't even allowed to see them. On top of that, not a single nurse or doctor had shown their face in over an hour to let him know just what the hell was going on. They had to have some information by now. He got up from his chair, stormed out of the cafeteria, and headed to the desk outside the ICU wing. Dennis's temper hit critical mass when he arrived at the nurses' station to find it empty and not a soul in the hallway either.

"Where the hell is everyone?" he called out.

The hall was silent. He walked down the wing into the ICU and called out again. "Hello, is anybody there?" He listened. "Where the hell is everybody, for Christ's sake?" Earlier, the door to his son's room had been open, but now it was closed. The cold fluorescent light crept from under the door. A shadow passed through it, causing Dennis to start. Someone was in the room. "Hello, nurse, doctor. What's going on? I want to see my damn kids."

Dennis felt his blood boil as heat flushed his face with rage. He threw open the door and stormed into the room. The bed was empty, and his son was gone. In fact, there was no one in the room at all. It didn't make any sense; he was sure he had seen someone moving about. He was positive.

He checked to the left and right of the door, but the room was so small there was really no need. A discolored stain saturated the center of the empty bed, soiled and wet from the boy's sweat. Dennis noticed the clumps of hair covering the pillow where his son had laid his head.

"What have you done to my boy?" he screamed. Then it hit him; the foul odor was consuming, hard, noxious, and oppressive. Dennis gagged and took a step backward.

"Where is my son?!" he howled into the empty room.

There was a shuffling sound, and then there was movement. He had enough time to realize something was above him just before it grabbed him by the throat.

Ben had gotten out of the bed as instructed. Had crawled across the floor on all fours, scurried up the wall, and clung to the ceiling, where he had waited. It dropped onto the man and dug into him with its newly grown teeth. Then it drained the vessel and added Dennis Richards to the collective.

Karin Boyle had been unable to sleep, even with the help of the valium. Bob sat in a chair beside the bed, attempting to comfort her. "I'm sure Dr. Ziegler will be along any second with some good news," he told her.

"I'm scared, Bob. He looked terrible. You saw him. What's wrong with our boy?" She had been crying nonstop since they arrived last night.

"I don't know, baby," he said, stroking her hair. "I don't know."

"I thought it was the flu; he only had a fever. He said he didn't feel good when he came home on Thursday, and I was so mad because he was late. I yelled at him and told him I was gonna give him the beating of his life." She tried to control her sobs but was unable. "Oh, Bob, what if—" She couldn't finish.

"Stop," he said. "Don't do that to yourself. You're a great mother, don't ever doubt that. You didn't do anything wrong. Rob loves you."

She felt guilty for being mad at her son. What if she never got the chance to say she was sorry? He had worked so hard, and the Halloween party was all he had talked about. Then he had gotten sick. Karin blamed herself for the whole thing. She wished she could go back to Thursday night when Rob had come home late. She would have done everything differently.

There was a knock at the door that startled them. Then Dr. Malcolm entered the room and smiled. "What's all this?" he said. "I think you should follow me. There's a young man who wants to see his parents."

Karin jumped out of bed, and Bob got up from the chair. "Is Rob okay? How is he?" Bob asked.

"Oh, God. Thank you," Karin cried. "Is it true, Dr. Malcolm? Is he going to be all right?"

Dr. Malcolm smiled and rubbed the back of his neck. "Well, why don't you come see for yourself," he said and exited the room.

Bob and Karin followed the chief of medicine down the hall toward the ICU. He opened the door and let them inside. They rushed in, and Dr. Malcolm slammed it behind them. Robert wasn't in the bed.

"What's going on here, Doctor?" Bob screamed and tried to turn the doorknob. It wouldn't move; someone was holding it shut from the other side. Whoever it was had to be as strong as a bull. It couldn't be Dr. Malcolm.

"Open this door, dammit." Bob pounded against it.

"Bob!" Karin cried. "Dear God!"

Bob turned around and was hit by a stench that scrambled his guts. The hot tang of rotted meat filled the room like vapor. Then he heard it, the furtive sound of malicious intent, like an angry hornet trapped in a Dr. Pepper can. Gooseflesh pricked his skin as the strange sound grew in intensity and the overpowering stink punched him in the face. He covered his mouth just as two figures jumped from the floor onto the bed. Bob knew immediately that one of them was his son. "No."

Robert's body had changed, morphed into something deformed, insectile. The second creature had gone through a similar disfigurement. It focused on Bob with dark, bulbous eyes and began to preen itself.

"Oh my God!" Karin screamed as the small creatures propelled themselves toward them. The couple tried to back out of the way, but their attackers were lightning-quick and had them before they could move.

Rob seized his mother by the throat with hands that had grown talons. His claws dug into Karin's flesh as he drove her to the floor. She heard Bob struggle for a moment and then only a terrible gurgling sound.

Rob landed on his mother's chest and fed on her consciousness. Karin felt the icy presence enter her brain and projected a final thought. *I'm sorry, Rob, please don't be mad at me. I love you.*

The Boyles were added to the brood.

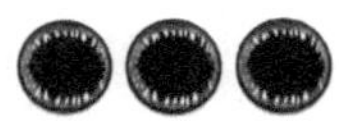

Carl and Burt drove back to the coroner's office, where a bottle of scotch waited for them. It wasn't going to make their problems go away, but it would make them a bit more bearable. Carl picked up the handset and spoke. "Leaving the foothills now. Did you find out anything yet, Andrea? Any word from Deputy Forsyth?" He prayed for at least a little good news.

"Affirmative, Sheriff," she replied. He let out a sigh of relief and waited for her to continue. "Deputy Forsyth dropped the squad car off about fifteen minutes ago. He got held up at Wilson's Diner. Apparently, Mandy Griggs had a little car trouble, and he gave her a ride home."

The men exchanged a smile. Everyone in town knew Mandy, and Carl had an idea there was a bit more to the story than Deputy Forsyth had told the dispatcher. He figured Gary would have a different tale to tell when it was just the guys.

"He never made it to the power plant," she continued, "said he'd head up there tomorrow."

"I'll bet," Burt said. Both men laughed.

"What about the kids? Did they leave their bikes in the woods today?"

"Kids said their bikes were stolen outside the A&P this morning. They came home late 'cause they were walking around town trying to find them and lost track of time." Andrea was full of good news.

"So, the case of the missing boys is solved." Carl smiled at Burt. "Someone left the bikes in the foothills. Tell the parents we found them behind the Richards house near the creek."

"Will do." She paused. "Sheriff, Dr. Malcolm called."

"He did?" Carl crossed his fingers, waiting for the other shoe to drop. This was where she would hit him with the bad news. "What did he say?"

"He said there's no need to worry, the children are showing signs of improvement, and there's no need to be concerned about contagion."

Carl eased against his seat and smiled. "That's great news." All Andrea had to do was tell him someone had found Felix Castillo's body, and most of his problems would be fixed. "Well, it certainly has been a long day."

"You can say that again, Sheriff. You need anything else?" she asked.

"Just a glass with some ice in it, dear." He laughed.

"Well, have one for me, Sheriff. Have a good night."

"I'll have two for you, Andrea. Good night." He returned the handset to the dashboard.

Burt tilted his head in question. "Guess the kids weren't as sick as he thought. Sounds promising."

"I'm surprised too. If you saw them last night, you would have said, no way. No way they would be doing better so soon. I guess Dr. Malcolm figured it out."

"Yeah, I guess so." Burt creased his brow.

"That only leaves us with one problem, Burt." Carl took a dig at his friend. "You realize how much trouble the two of us are looking at, don't you?"

"You think I don't know?" Burt shook his head. "I still can't explain it any other way than someone playing a sick joke. It's almost Halloween, you know?"

"Well, don't think different of me for bringing this up." Carl paused and thought carefully about what he was about to say. "If I report this like I should, you're bound to lose your job. I'll get my ass reamed, but the state will surely see you swing, buddy."

"Yeah, I was wondering how long it would take you to mention that."

Carl let out an exaggerated exhale. "I can't believe I'm about to say this, and if any of it leaves this car, I'll deny every word."

"What are you trying to say, Carl?"

"This guy Castillo didn't have any family, no next of kin. Maybe I don't have to make that call just yet. Let's see if the body turns up. It's not like anyone's coming in to identify him."

"I can't let you put your ass on the line like that," Burt told him.

"I really don't see how you have much of a choice. If I call it in now, you'll lose your job and probably your pension along with it." Carl paused for dramatic effect and to let his friend realize the magnitude of the situation.

"Now, if we wait and the body never shows up ... God forbid, you fill out the autopsy report and burn it."

"Huh ... burn what?" Burt asked.

The Sheriff continued. "You turn on the incinerator, and I don't care what you burn. Burn that damn suit you wear every day. I will report that we have no leads, and it becomes a cold case, and that's that. Now, if by some miracle the body does show up, then I will call you and let you know that we found the body you reported stolen. I can't believe I am saying this, but I don't feel like I have much of a choice."

"Carl, I—"

"Listen, old man, you worked for my father when he was sheriff, and you've always been a good friend. I wouldn't do this for anyone else in the world. But I can't stand by and watch you lose your job and retirement just for being, I don't know ... a really irresponsible coroner."

"That's fair," he said. "I deserve it."

"Right now, we're going to go back to that lab, you're gonna break out that bottle, and we're gonna get drunk. Who knows, maybe Felix Castillo will be there waiting for us, and you can buy him a drink too."

"I don't know what to say, Carl." Burt rubbed his eyes.

"Well, don't say anything yet because I could still change my mind."

"You're a good friend, Carl. Thank you."

"Like I said, Burt," he looked at his friend, "I could still change my mind."

Sally Ann Richards finally managed to fall asleep, thanks to the valium Dr. Ziegler prescribed. The staff had allowed her and Dennis to rest in one of the unoccupied rooms on the same floor as the ICU ward. Unfortunately, they were still not allowed into the room with their kids and were only able to see them from as close as the doorway, since Dr. Malcolm was still concerned about contagion.

But Sally Ann couldn't understand why she was being prevented from seeing her children. If she was going to get sick, surely, she would have already. She'd been with them round-the-clock since they first came down with fevers. Poor little Erin was losing her teeth. It was horrible. Sally Ann was helpless to do anything, and on top of that, she was thoroughly exhausted. She hadn't slept at all, except for the few minutes before Erin came to her in the living room and vomited.

Now, thanks to the tiny blue pill Dr. Ziegler had given her, she slept restlessly, tossing and turning, falling in and out of consciousness. Dennis had turned the lights out before heading to the cafeteria, leaving the room dark and quiet. The only light was from the streetlamps in the parking lot. It filtered through the blinds, casting long shadows against the far wall.

Sally had been plagued by repeated visions from the previous night. In her dream, she was asleep in her bedroom on Mountain Ave. But then she was suddenly expelled into wakefulness by an urgent need to tend to her children, who were sick and in pain. Although she would try to be quiet as she left the bed where Dennis lay sleeping, every step she made on the hallway floor felt as loud as hammers on concrete. No matter how careful she tried to be, she would either trip over something in the hall or knock over a table. At which point, Dennis would charge from the bedroom, screaming, and start to shake her. That's when Sally would wake up, confused and unsure of where she was. Until she recognized the shadows on the far wall and remembered she was still in the center and her babies were so sick. Then, laying her head back down against the pillow, the valium would kick in, and the dream would start all over again. Repeatedly, she would find herself back in her own bed, lost in the spin cycle.

Sally had just awoken from the nightmare and looked around the unfamiliar dark room. *Where am I?* Confusion dominated for a moment, but soon she realized where she was: still at Chilton, exhausted and completely drained. Then ... she heard it, faint and gentle like the movement of fabric on flesh. There was a soft rustle near the door of the room, and Sally thought Dennis must be sitting in the dark and had fallen asleep himself.

"Den, what time is it?" she called to him.

There was another soft rustle that almost sounded like paper being dragged across the floor. The sound drew closer to where Sally Ann lay.

Rustle ... Scrape ... Rustle.

"Dennis, is that you?" Sally's eyes focused on a small shadow as it approached the side of her bed. Then the shadow spoke.

"Mommy ... I don't feel so good," Erin whispered in a garbled voice that was no longer human.

To be continued ...

The Ojanox Book II: Ashes to Ashes

Coming 8/6/2024

Thank you for reading!
Please consider leaving a rating/review on Goodreads and Amazon.

Continue reading The Ojanox Book II: Ashes to Ashes

Download a free excerpt from Ashes to Ashes

The Ojanox Series: Books 1 - 4

The Ojanox Series is now available at Amazon and Barnes & Noble.

ACKNOWLEDGEMENTS

If you ever find yourself in the town of Pompton Plains, New Jersey, and drive to the very top of Mountain Avenue, you will reach Mountainside Park, but you won't find an old road extension or an abandoned sanatorium. However, the inspiration for the old hospital comes from a place called the Overbrook, which wasn't all that far away. Neither is the real Garrett Mountain, for that matter. I took great liberties when writing this book, even changing the location to upstate New York, but many of the features are similar to the town I grew up in: Chilton medical center, the graveyard behind the Lutheran Church, even the hardware store at the corner of Jackson Ave. I just changed things a little to fit the story.

It's been four years since I first started writing this book, and there are many who helped bring this monster to life. Whether their assistance was inspirational, fact-checking, information gathering, or emotional support, I couldn't have done this without them. There are topics I touched on in *The Ojanox* that required the input of professionals and tons of research. When it comes to toxicology, lab work, virology, and bacteriology, I did my best to stick to the facts. When I got it wrong—when faced with serving the story or the hard medical facts, I chose the story. So that's on me.

First, I would like to thank Wendy Nastasi and my sister, Dawn Chiossi (Danielle), for a lifetime of inspiration, support, and for listening to me talk about nothing other than this damn book for the past three years. I would also like to thank them for lending their namesakes to this story, with written consent, of course.

There are several friends who read early versions of this book whose help was instrumental. Nick Gomes and Ed Koloski helped provide feedback and were my sounding board from the very start, back in the halfway house days. Greg Gillick and Mike Turrigiano have always had my back and were there to listen to my very first attempts at horror writing. And of course, Jack Wells. Jack has been my constant go-to guy with this project for years. He read it before the first rewrite, and he still came back for more. Now that's a true friend. In truth, *The Ojanox* wouldn't be half the book it is today without Jack's knowledge, skill, and literary prowess.

My editor, Lisa Lee Tone, took every page of this manuscript and made it better with her diligent attention to detail. I'm fortunate to have Lisa in my corner to call me out when I stray from the path, and I'm thankful she was always there to rope me back in.

I'd like to thank Ben Eads for his original developmental edits on *Scream in the Dark* and for the rigorous Jedi training and instruction. (Insert Yoda voice) Because of you, a better writer, I am.

Christy Aldridge has been so much more than a cover artist, or an illustrator, or even a contributor—she has been a partner, in every sense of the word. Without Christy's hard work and dedication, this project wouldn't be half of what it is today. For the past year or more, we have been joined at the hip. She took my vision and brought it to life. Thank you, Christy, I couldn't have done this without you. Now we need to start a new project.

Thank you, Don Noble and Jeff DeSantis for contributing your amazing illustrations and talents to this project.

Many thanks to my Alpha team and proofreaders for their time, input, and suggestions: Donna Latham, Heather Ann Larson, Jae Mazer, Kerrie Roylance, Bryan Moyer, Kristen Lynch, Susan Isenberg, John O'regan, Christina Marie, Kira (Eagle Eyes) Seamon, and Maryanne Pacheco Chappell.

For all my friends who follow me on social media, for all the reviewers, bloggers, influencers who support the indie horror community, thank you. Also, thank you Tiffany Koplin, RJ Roles, and all the admins at the Books of Horror Facebook group for everything you do.

My life would have been very different if it hadn't been for my fourth-grade teacher, Mrs. Genevieve Smith, whose tutelage, undying devotion, and wealth of limitless stories molded not only myself but an entire generation. I especially would like to thank you for bringing my homework to the hospital when I broke my leg.

Thank you, Kelly Rainey, and all the fourth-grade classes of Pompton Plains school.

Anthony Lorraine helped by sharing with me his experiences in Vietnam. Without Anthony, the character of Carl Primrose would have been much different, as well as my knowledge of that moment in history. Sadly, I learned of Anthony's passing when I was still in the halfway house. He was a good friend during a dark moment in my life. I miss you, Tony.

Thank you to my family and friends who helped contribute to the inspiration of this story through a lifetime of experiences, which I in turn felt compelled to fictionalize. And finally, for my mom, who told me my first ghost story, took me trick-or-treating, and allowed me to have a Halloween party at the house when I was ten years old. And for my dad, who let me build a haunted house and still reminds me periodically that I painted his garage walls black.

And thank you to the readers and horror fans who love this genre as much as I do. Thank you for taking this journey with me and thank you for allowing me to share this story with you. I hope you enjoyed it half as much as I enjoyed writing it.

Daemon Manx

ABOUT THE AUTHOR

Daemon Manx is an American author with a backstory. He is a recovering addict who spent nearly a decade in the prison system where he focused on recovery and learned to perfect his horror writing craft. He has been featured in magazines in both the U.S., the U.K, and Germany. In 2021 he received a HAG award for his story *The Dead Girl* and was nominated for a Splatterpunk award that same year.

He was a bonus round winner on the gameshow *Wheel of Fortune* in 1999 and is infamously known for a motor vehicle accident he was responsible for, involving President Ronald Reagan's limousine.

After struggling with addiction and incarceration, Daemon now has over eleven years clean and sober. He uses his story to illustrate the positive outcome of sobriety and offer a glimpse at what life can be like when one receives a second chance.

He lives with his sister, author Danielle Manx and their narcoleptic cat, Sydney, where they patiently prepare for the apocalypse. There is a good chance they will run out of coffee far too soon.

242